Up and Down the Scratchy Mountains

OR

*The Search for
a Suitable Princess*

by LAUREL SNYDER

pictures by GREG CALL

A YEARLING BOOK

Text copyright © 2008 by Laurel Snyder
Illustrations copyright © 2008 by Greg Call

All rights reserved. Published in the United States by Yearling, an imprint of Random House Children's Books, a division of Random House, Inc., New York. Originally published in hardcover in the United States by Random House Children's Books, a division of Random House, Inc., New York, in 2008.

Yearling and the jumping horse design are registered trademarks of Random House, Inc.

Visit us on the Web! www.randomhouse.com/kids

Educators and librarians, for a variety of teaching tools, visit us at www.randomhouse.com/teachers

The Library of Congress has cataloged the hardcover edition of this work as follows:
Snyder, Laurel.
Up and down the Scratchy Mountains, or, The search for a suitable princess / Laurel Snyder ; illustrated by Greg Call.
p. cm.
Summary: Lucy, a milkmaid, and her best friend Wynston, a reluctant prince, go in search of information about Lucy's missing mother—even though Wynston is supposed to be searching for a proper princess to marry.
ISBN 978-0-375-84719-6 (trade) — ISBN 978-0-375-94719-3 (lib. bdg.) —
ISBN 978-0-375-84720-2 (pbk.) — ISBN 978-0-375-84990-9 (e-book)
[1. Fairy tales.] I. Call, Greg, ill. II. Title. III. Title: Search for a suitable princess.
PZ8.S4177Up 2008
[Fic]—dc22
2007015689

Printed in the United States of America

10 9 8 7 6 5 4 3 2

First Yearling Edition

*This book is for
Mose and Lewis.
My boys.*
—L.S.

CONTENTS

(Before the Beginning Began) 1

In the Village of Thistle 9

Beyond the Village 34

Cat the Dog and Willie Wimple 55

The Short Cut, the Long Cut,
    and the Curious Storm 75

A Very Civilized Place 101

Wild Ravening Beasts 122

No Room for Wiggling 142

The End of the Rope 157

Down and Down and Further Down . . . 183

Heading Home, and Arriving 208

(After, and After That) 230

Up and Down the Scratchy Mountains

(BEFORE THE BEGINNING BEGAN)

OUR STORY doesn't begin *Once upon a time* or *Back in the days of yore*. It didn't happen as long ago as all that, but still it happened before televisions and interstate highways, and even before your grandma was a little girl. Back then, the world was a different place.

Nowadays people can visit anywhere they please, because of silver airplanes and big ocean liners. Nowadays people can go to France or Zimbabwe, Topeka or Kathmandu, and be home in time for dinner. But back when this story began, the world had tiny corners—pockets nobody ever visited because it was too hard to get there.

In one such corner of the world, beyond two continents and across a wide ocean (nowhere near France or Topeka), there was a corner of the world that was chock-

full of rolling hills and jagged mountains, rivers and streams, and walled villages. And in that land, which was called the Bewilderness, there was a village called Thistle. And just inside the village walls of Thistle there was a blue barn. And beside the barn—close enough that the red-and-white cows sometimes munched on the window-box geraniums—there was a tiny house.

It was a stone house—a white one—with a thatched roof and a smokestack that chuffed cheerfully. In the house there was a family that consisted of a papa, a mama, and two little girls named Sally and Lucy. The family was happy almost all of the time, which is as happy as anyone can really expect to be.

Sally was only two years old, but she was helpful, quiet, and well behaved. Her brown hair hung straight and was never mussed, and somehow her shoes stayed remarkably clean. Everything about Sally was clean—in fact, her very favorite game of all was *helping Mama fold the dish towels*, which is unusual for a child. Sally was *good*.

Lucy was *not*. She was a tiny baby—fresh and bright and snappy, with a peach glow and a head of rosy curls—but she screamed all the time. She screamed when she was being put to sleep and when she was waking up, and sometimes she even screamed when she was snoring. She screamed when she was eating mashed peas, so that the peas fell out of her mouth in a blurp. She screamed when her papa chucked her under the chin and when he left in the morning to milk the cows. And she screamed loudest whenever Sally tried to hold her, because Sally's arms were too small. So sometimes Lucy slid free and landed with a thunk on the floor.

In fact, the only time that Lucy didn't scream was when her mama held her in the rocker and sang to her softly. Since nobody liked to hear Lucy scream, her mama sang to her most of the day, and often at night. She sang every song she knew, and some she didn't really know. When she ran out of songs to sing, she made up tunes of her own and sang the words from her cookbook:

> *Oh, take two cups of sugar,*
> *And put 'em in a pot,*
> *Then add a bunch of raisins,*
> *And stir it up a lot.*
> *When it gets to bubbling,*
> *Chop an apple in,*
> *And now I can't remember*
> *Where I put my rolling pin!*

When her voice wore out, she hummed. And Lucy listened and cooed all the while. But Lucy's favorite song, the song that put her right to sleep every single time, was a song that her mama had learned when she was a little girl herself, before she came to live in Thistle. The song that Lucy loved so dearly and so quietly was a song that the goatherds sang on the slopes of the Scratchy Mountains. Lucy's mama called it the "Song of the Mountain," and it went like this:

> *Though winter snows may freeze us,*
>   *and spring storms flood our beds,*
> *We're glad to feel the mountain grass*
>   *is pillowing our heads.*
> *Though goats may be our closest friends,*
>   *and life is simple here,*
> *We like it on the mountain,*
>   *where the air is sharp and clear.*
> *We have no use for fancy things,*
>   *so keep your lace and jams.*
> *We have no need for company,*
>   *just labor for our hands.*
> *And goats to sleep beside us,*
>   *and bread to keep us full.*

4

And stars above to guide us,
  and blankets made of wool.
We think of you with kindly thoughts,
  but seek the simple life.
We choose the mountain over
  all the joys of hearth and wife.
We've felt the sun from heaven,
  and breathed the mountain air
And now it seems that city life
  is too much life to bear.

By the time Lucy was one year old, she no longer needed to be sung to sleep every four minutes. She had discovered that there were other kinds of trouble to make and that most trouble was best executed in silence. So she stopped screaming and began crawling, eating bugs, opening cupboard doors, and pulling on her mother's skirts. She was no less trouble, but at least she was quieter. In fact, she never made a peep.

Each day her parents tried to coax her to speak. Her mama would lean over her and whisper, "Mama? Papa? Blankie?" And Lucy would look up at her mother and open her lips as if she wanted to speak. But then her little mouth would snap shut defiantly, and she'd return to pulling the dog's ears or chewing on a chair leg. Her father would toss her in the air, hoping to hear her scream, but it never worked. Usually she just drooled on him.

Lucy never spoke at all. She was silent as a stone until one night when she was two years old. Lucy's mama was putting her girls to bed, and as she tucked them in, she began to sing the goatherd song. "Though winter snows may freeze us . . . ," she began.

Suddenly Lucy sat bolt-upright in bed and opened her mouth. ". . . and spring storms flood our beds," she sang in a warbling little-girl voice.

Lucy's mama shrieked and clapped her hands to her mouth. Sally shrieked too, and Lucy's papa came running from the next room. "Hello? What's all this screaming about?"

Lucy's mother pointed and stammered, but Lucy kept right on singing. She had never said *Papa* or *Mama*. She had never said *yes* or *no* or *dog* or *cat* or *Lucy* or *uh-oh*. She had never uttered a word, but now she was making up for lost time. Lucy sang the entire song from memory as her family stared in surprise. When she was done, she lay back down, stuck her thumb in her mouth, and closed her eyes. She had sung herself to sleep.

In the long silence that followed, Sally turned over

. . . she'd return to pulling the dog's ears . . .

like the good four-year-old girl that she was and went to sleep. But then, the very next day, *something terrible* happened. To Lucy and Sally, who barely remembered, and to their poor papa, who could never forget.

Yes, in the time shortly after *Once upon a time*—in the little white stone house beside the blue barn—in the village of Thistle—in a corner of the world known as the Bewilderness—in the shadow of the Scratchy Mountains, where the goatherds sang—something terrible happened.

Just as it was getting dark, and with no warning whatsoever . . . Mama was there, and then . . . she was *gone.*

IN THE VILLAGE OF THISTLE

MANY YEARS passed, because that is what happens, even when something very sad has taken place. It is the nature of years to pass, and the nature of little girls to grow. Sally and Lucy grew tall and strong and very busy, with birthdays and chores, sneezes and haircuts, school and snowstorms. Sally and Lucy learned to swim and read and bake cookies. Just like you.

Lucy grew to be the loveliest little milkmaid in the village of Thistle, or anywhere else in the Bewilderness. She had striking red corkscrew curls that danced wildly down her back. She had exceedingly long lashes that fringed the biggest, bluest eyes you've ever seen. Her cheeks were pink, but her skin everywhere else was the creamy white of the milk in her milk pails. And she moved quick like a feather—dipping and swinging her buckets as she went, in a kind of dance. From a distance, Lucy seemed just perfect.

But sometimes our outsides do not quite match our insides. This was indeed the case with Lucy. Because underneath her skirts, Lucy's knees were scratched and scraped from tree climbing and puddle jumping. And when she opened her mouth, people meeting her for the first time were always startled by the sharp tone of her voice. There was no way around it—Lucy was *bossy*.

Lucy's best friend was a boy named Wynston. He happened to be a prince, but that wasn't his fault. It also wasn't his fault that his ears stuck out or that he was a little too thin and tall for his feet, so that he often stumbled over himself. Lucy didn't mind.

Lucy and Wynston spent most of their days together. They wandered through wide fields of goldenrod, sneezing where they walked. They gathered bird eggs in the hills and they paddled in the river, where tiny silver fish tickled their ankles. They swung on vines, sang silly songs, and argued. They enjoyed arguing, and they were very good at it.

Often their arguments revolved around how Wynston didn't like to get his shoes muddy or stain his breeches, which Lucy found utterly silly. She'd wrinkle her nose, toss her long red curls, and laugh at him.

"You know, Wynston, some princes journey to far-away lands in great sailing vessels, or tromp through frozen wastelands in search of magical beasts—but noooo, not you. You wouldn't want to upset your papa by spoiling your best vest!"

Wynston had been raised in the castle and trained to keep himself tidy, so there were limits to just how messy he'd get. Lucy, on the other hand, took great pride in her stained skirts and ran barefoot whenever she could get away with it, which was often.

But cleanliness wasn't all that Lucy and Wynston fought about, not at all. They argued about *everything*, about whether the field was greener than it had been the day before, and about whether the moon followed the sun or the sun followed the moon. Lucy and Wynston argued about what to eat for lunch, but not until after they'd finished arguing about where to eat it.

Every day, when Lucy met Wynston at the cobbled corner of Mill Road and Willow Way, she stuck out her milkmaid tongue and said (in her sharp, loud voice) something like, "You're slower than a sleepy snail on a cold morning, slower than a turtle in the road!"

And every day Wynston tapped her on the nose and replied, "I can't help it if your father's a jackrabbit and your mother was a hummingbird." Then he straightened the thin circlet of gold he was, by law, required to wear on his head at all times. Or he pushed aside his floppy brown bangs. Or he tucked in his purple velvet shirt. (Later, when he wasn't looking, Lucy usually untucked it in the back, because she could.)

Most days, Lucy's sister, Sally, complained that Lucy and Wynston gave her a headache with their bickering. Wynston's royal father, King Desmond, just shook his chubby royal finger and said in his most royal voice, "Wynston, my boy, this isn't fitting for a prince."

Wynston smarted when his father said such things, but King Desmond was cranky about almost everything Wynston did, so Wynston didn't always listen. Certainly he didn't listen when the sun was sunning and the fields were fielding. Not with Lucy waiting at the gate with her tin lunch pail, tapping her toe impatiently and squinting her blue eyes against the sun. "Oh, Wynston, do you ask your father for permission to use the bathroom too?"

These sun-drenched days passed pleasantly, and became weeks, which turned into months. But with each season, Lucy had a little more milk to deliver and more butter to churn in the creamery behind the barn. Meanwhile, Wynston had new royal duties. He learned how to count the chests of gold in the tower and how to sign his name with big swirly letters in purple ink. By the time he was twelve, he'd learned how to properly shine rubies against his shirt, and precisely when to look disapproving. His father had even shown him the hidden doors to the secret passageways in the cellar, though nobody could remember where they went.

Then one Saturday Wynston was practicing his royal walk on the stone staircase. King Desmond cleared his throat, patted his brocaded belly, twisted his impressive silver mustache, and said, "Ahem! Wynston, my boy, the time has come."

"For what?" asked Wynston.

"For what?" repeated the king with a hint of humor in his blustery voice. He ran his fingers, which flashed with gold and diamonds, through his thinning hair. "For what? For life! For you to grow up, my lad."

"Grow up?"

"Yes indeed! All the ruby-shining in the world won't make you a good king if you haven't got a suitable queen, and a suitable queen begins as a suitable princess."

"But I'm only twelve," said Wynston, "and I've kind

of got my hands full right now, with lessons and lectures and practices. Besides, I've got *forever* to think about queens." His voice wobbled and threatened to crack.

"That's what you think," answered the king impatiently. "Why, with all the various negotiations, meetings, royal visitations, contracts, and tournaments—not to mention the party-planning that your aunt's got to take care of—it'll be a good seven or eight years before we can turn a prospective princess into a suitable wife for you. And if you decide on a foreign girl, say, from Flandeurestine, or Montrapucinonininonino, and she has to learn our language, you can add another two or three years to the process. So we better get cracking now."

"I guess you're right," said Wynston, feeling a little nervous. "I guess I didn't realize—"

"Of *course* you didn't . . . ," the king interrupted.

"But I suppose you're right. . . ."

"Of *course* I am, but it's nice that we're in agreement. Handy, since I've already made arrangements for you to meet with a princess this week. Halcyon is her name."

"So fast?" Wynston made a face and scrunched his nose in an odd lopsided way.

"Yes, my boy. Right away. It's time to get down to the business of Queening!"

Wynston looked up from his curtsy and nodded his head. But when he did, he lost his balance, stumbled on a crooked stair, and fell in a heap on the dusty floor. The king, his head full of plans and contracts, just stepped over Wynston as he made his way up the stairs. Wynston stayed on the floor until dinner, thinking about queens and princesses, and feeling bewildered. He didn't even move when a mouse scurried past his nose.

The next day, Lucy couldn't find Wynston. He wasn't waiting at the crossroads as usual. So Lucy stopped at the back door of the castle on her way to pick blackberries, but Masha the cook shook her head. "Sorry, my love. I haven't seen Wynston anywhere. And there's strange business in the castle—itchy business."

"But it's Sunday!" said Lucy. "We always go berrying on Sunday, and Wynston knows I need his help—for carrying all the berries, and in case there's a wasp or something. Plus, he knows I hate to go by myself."

"You get a little lonely, my sweetums?"

"That's not why!" exclaimed Lucy, though she blushed as she said it.

"Oh, Lucy, there's no need for embarrassment," said

Masha. "Nobody likes to be lonely. But even so, I can't stand here chattering today. I've got to dust the dustbins, shine the curtains, and polish the cats. And the king wants fourteen different kinds of pie. Fourteen!"

"Fourteen kinds of pie?" said Lucy. "What could anyone possibly need with fourteen kinds of pie?"

"I'm sure I don't know," said Masha. "When I asked him, he said, 'Well, Masha, we need every flavor you can think up, since we don't know what kind they like over there.' Over *where* is what I'd like to know. As if there's a place where folks don't like a nice cherry pie. A crazy place that'd be! Nevertheless, I need to make the pies, so if you'd be so kind as to bring me any extra blackberries you find, they'd be appreciated." Masha wandered away, knotting her apron strings in frustration and mumbling, "Lemon, apple, mince, strawberry-rhubarb, rhubarb-strawberry. Oh heavens!"

Lucy sat on the castle gate to think for a minute, and two fat tears began to roll down her cheeks. She rubbed them away furiously, but they came right back. Lucy hated to cry! Usually, she could make up a song or think of a silly face Wynston had made and the tears would stop. Only, today no songs were coming to her, and Wynston was the last person she needed to think about.

So she balled up her fists, hopped down from the fence, and marched away with a sense of purpose. She wouldn't let him ruin her Sunday.

The only problem was that when Lucy was feeling cranky, she always talked to Wynston. Now that she was fussy at Wynston, there was nobody to talk to. She tried to think of who might listen to her frustrations, but nobody came to mind.

Sally? Sally was *boooring*, and prissy besides. Papa? A girl couldn't talk about feelings like this to her father, especially not Lucy's quiet, stern father, however nice he was on the inside. No, there was really nobody to talk to . . . nobody at all. Lucy felt . . . lonely.

"If only my mother were here, I wouldn't need Wynston at all," Lucy said to a gray squirrel carrying an acorn. "Yes, Mama would know what to do about a goofy prince."

The squirrel looked doubtful.

"Yes, she would so too," added Lucy indignantly. "Mamas are very good for talking, and feelings, and stuff . . . or that's what I've heard anyway."

The squirrel ran off.

So Lucy picked up her pail and walked to the blackberry patch alone, where she stuffed herself until her mouth was purple. She rolled in the sun-warmed grass and kicked through the burbling stream, but it was very quiet without Wynston. At the end of the day, she sat on a hill to watch the sun set behind the castle. Then she brushed off her skirts and walked down the hill with her pail, heavy and brimming with dark berries. She left it on the steps of the castle and went home for supper, where Sally and Papa were waiting patiently.

But when she sat down at the table, Lucy just pushed a mound of beans around her plate noisily and grumped.

"Lucy!" said her papa firmly. He covered her little hand with his own hand. It felt rough, lined with the hard work of milking. "That's not how we eat our supper, is it? What a terrible noise! Don't you have any manners at all?"

"Hmph!" Lucy hmphed at her papa. "I don't suppose I do. And I don't suppose it really matters."

She continued to scrape at her beans. Then she stuck out her tongue at Sally and threw her spoon on the floor. She didn't know what had come over her. She could feel the grumpiness taking control of her hands. She knew she was being dreadful but couldn't stop.

"Lucy!" Her father's stern voice grew sterner. "You are now excused from the table. And I don't want to hear a peep out of you until the end of dinner."

"I don't care," snarked Lucy, pushing back her chair

so that it made a loud *scrreeeeeech* on the floor. "I don't want to talk to *you* anyway. So there."

"And no singing either," her father said coldly. "And no writing in your diary."

"Oh, that's just perfect," answered Lucy tartly. "You're silent all day long, and now I have to be silent too."

"What?" Lucy's father was confused.

"You won't talk about things, and now I can't either." She stomped from the room.

"What was *that* all about?" Lucy heard her papa asking Sally in a bewildered tone. Lucy went to bed in her clothes. She sprawled angrily on the quilt and stared at the ceiling for hours. She knew she'd made a fuss for no reason, but she was too grumpy to feel bad about it.

The next morning Sally and Lucy walked to the market as usual, but Lucy was still in a bad mood. She sucked intently on a ringlet of her hair as she stomped her feet to town.

Sally looked at the wet, slimy strand of hair in her sister's hand and frowned. "You know, Lucy, that really isn't very becoming." Sally never sucked her hair. Sally's skirts were always crisp and clean, and her shining brown locks were always tucked neatly into a headband that perfectly matched her shoes.

Lucy paused for a second as though listening to Sally, but then she asked a question, a big question. "Sally, what do you think happened to Mama?"

There was a long silence before Sally spoke. When she did, it was in a calm, careful voice.

"You know I don't have an answer for that, Lucy. Papa doesn't talk about it, so how could I know?"

"But shouldn't you . . . I mean, we . . . wonder? I mean, wouldn't you like to know?"

Sally sighed. "Some things are like that, Lucy. I don't know how the morning glories know to close at night. I don't know why cream rises in the milk pail. There are a lot of things I don't know. That's just how life is."

"But don't you miss her?"

Sally sighed even more deeply. "How can I miss what I barely remember?"

"Well, I miss her, even though I don't remember her at all. I miss all the things she would have done with me and all the things we would have talked about. I feel like a puzzle with missing pieces."

Sally squirmed uncomfortably and shook her head. "It's better not to talk about it."

"Why?"

"It just is. It's easier not to think about it."

"Not for me."

"If Papa wanted us to know, he'd tell us. And if he doesn't want to talk about it, why should we?"

"But that's just the problem. . . . Nobody wants to talk about it," said Lucy. Sally picked up her stride and moved quickly down the path, away from her sister and the difficult question.

Lucy felt frustrated. She knew Sally and she were different kinds of people, but without Wynston to talk to, Sally was all she had. Lucy had always spent so much time with the prince, she'd never bothered to make friends with any of the girls at school. She'd always thought they were silly, fussy, and too tidy, like Sally. But now, for the first time, she thought maybe this had been a mistake. Still, there was nothing she could do about it today. Oh, why didn't Sally want to know about Mama? Why didn't Sally feel the *mystery*, the longing she felt?

Lucy wanted to mull the subject over for a little longer, but already Sally was far ahead. So Lucy had to give up thinking thoughts and run to catch up. A minute later, walking in stride with Sally again, she returned to sucking on her hair.

Suddenly Sally whirled around and said in an un-usually loud un-Sally-ish voice, "You *really* shouldn't do that, you know. Sucking on your hair is germy and icky and ew. I swear, I don't know how Wynston puts up with you all the time!"

At that, Lucy stopped sucking on her hair long enough to set down her basket. "Geez. How come you're so mad? And what made you say that about Wynston?" Lucy demanded.

"No reason," quickly replied Sally, who was never loud for long. "I was just feeling angry. Sorry. I didn't mean to lose my temper."

"That's okay, but seriously, what made you mention Wynston?"

"I don't know. What's the big deal about Wynston?"

"No big deal," said Lucy, looking at Sally carefully.

"You're ridiculous," said Sally as she tossed her perfect head perfectly. So Lucy explained, a bit.

"I'm feeling a little . . . odd . . . about Wynston. He stood me up," she said.

But Sally was no help. "Oh, pooh. Likely he was off at a lesson, learning to groom his father's ferns or some such silliness."

She continued on her way, and Lucy stared after her.

"Come *on!*" called Sally over her shoulder. "We'll be late for market." Sally hated to be late for anything, even her chores.

But Lucy didn't care. She left her basket where it was and started the other way down the path. She'd had a thought! She finally knew whom she could talk to about Wynston . . . someone who might be able to help her understand.

She hurtled down the path and turned left at the fork in the road that led to the royal estate. She pattered over the moat bridge and up the stone steps of the castle. Then she rang the huge attendance bell and went to wait in the Great Hall for the king to arrive.

She sat on a stiff stone chair big enough for a gigantic giant. The hall was cold and empty, so Lucy whispered into the huge room, "Wynston?" But the room ate her voice, so she spent a few minutes craning her neck and peering at the enormous map that hung above her head, a map of the Bewilderness. Finally she turned herself around to face the wall behind her. She perched on her knees to get a better look.

Just above her left shoulder she found Thistle, with the castle at its center. And just above Thistle she could make out the dark, treacherous peaks of the Scratchy Mountains,

. . . she spent a few minutes peering at the enormous map . . .

dotted with cliffs and crags. They stretched to the very top of the map, and seemed impassible. But the first mountain was a little different, backlit with sunbeams and encircled by a bright blue river. It looked . . . fascinating.

But staring at the old map, however beguiling, was cold comfort in the Great Hall. So Lucy turned back around in her seat, away from the map, and tried her usual cheer-up trick. She sang a song, and she swung her legs as she sang:

Oh, the larks and the rain and the little bitty bees,
all sniffle and snuffle in the tall, tall trees.
They much prefer to be down with the roses,
on the low, low branches near the big trees' toeses.

Lucy's voice was small and clear, and it echoed in the room, scaring her a little. Just then King Desmond entered. He was wiping his shirt with a handkerchief and muttering, "My, my goodness, and gravy to boot—" He hurried over to Lucy.

She was sitting so high that the king's nose was just level with her bare swinging feet. "Hello, Lucy. I'm afraid I'm in something of a muddle today. Not much time to spare, and I seem to have gotten a dribble on my best shirt. Cloth of gold—oh my! Perhaps you could come back on Thursday? Thursday is a splendid day for visiting. Masha makes brownies. . . ."

Lucy shook her curls. "No, King Desmond. I need to talk to you now. It's just—well, I always meet Wynston on Sunday mornings for our usual scamper. Then yesterday he didn't come down, and Masha said he was too busy. But what I want to ask you is . . . is Wynston mad at me? I thought you might know." She looked down at the king from her high perch and waited for an answer.

"Maybe he forgot," offered the king, picking at the gravy on his shirt.

"But we always meet on Sunday. Every Sunday since we were five years old! I don't see how he could possibly forget." Lucy shook her head. "He must be mad at me."

"Oh, Lucy, my girl. He isn't angry so far as I know, but—" The king sighed. "How shall I say this?" He leaned against the giant chair. "Lucy, we are all very fond of you, but the time has come for Wynston to turn his mind to matters of state and circumstance, to ruby-shining and princess-finding and the like."

"Princess-finding?" echoed Lucy and the Great Hall.

"Yes, we rather need to find him a suitable princess. That takes a lot of time, since suitable princesses are scarce these days, and most of them are silly girls with too much hair who take endless dancing lessons and long naps."

"But I don't understand why he needs a princess to begin with."

"Well, a king must have a queen. That's the way it goes." When he said the word *queen*, the king looked sadly across the throne room at a portrait on the wall. An oil painting of a thin woman with an extraordinary amount of hair hung in a heavy gilded frame. "It's a sad thing, a king without a queen." He sighed. "I miss Germantrude every single day . . . since I lost her."

"Yes, it's very sad and all, and I'm sorry for your loss, of course, but you do all right," said Lucy. "You seem to be just fine without a queen."

"Oh, but my child, I'm not. It isn't the same, sitting on that high throne by myself. And while I'm extremely lucky to have my sister around to fill in at luncheons and other queenly occasions . . . it isn't the same." He walked to the painting and ran his finger along the frame.

"No, I suppose not," answered Lucy, who didn't think much of Lavinia, the king's sister. Lavinia was always trying to organize Lucy's curls. And when she wasn't, she was mostly napping or eating cream puffs.

She gave the king a minute before she interrupted.

"So what's the big deal, then? Wynston needs a queen, and you'll find him one. What's so hard about that?"

The king woke from his reverie and stepped away from his beloved Germantrude. "Ah—it's not so easy. It takes a lot of time, as I said. So I'm guessing that while you were waiting for him yesterday, he was studying his lessons or going through the directory."

"The directory?"

"The directory of suitable hands, of course! It's a lot of reading, and you have to pay careful attention, because the writing is very small and the pictures aren't always exactly accurate."

"Pictures?"

"Yes, pictures of all the hands."

"Hands?"

"Hands in marriage, of course." The king sighed again. "I forget how little common people know about royal matters of state. You've heard of asking for a girl's hand in marriage?"

"Of course."

"You can tell a lot about a girl, you know, simply by looking at her hands."

"Oh," said Lucy, trying not to glance at her own chewed fingernails and grubby palms. "I see."

"Good!" The king was pleased.

"But if it's such a lot of work, couldn't *I* just be his suitable princess?"

"How sweet," chuckled the king. "You long to be the princess of Thistle? To wear a crown of gold? To marry my noble son?"

Lucy wrinkled her nose in a funny way. "Not especially," she replied. "I'm rather fond of being just who I am, but I'm not pleased at missing romps with my best friend because he has to curtsy with a bunch of snippy-nosed twit-nits with yellow hair and tight shoes!"

The king crossed his arms. "*Harumph!* They don't *all* have yellow hair. And just as Wynston has learned to be a king by watching me, so a suitable princess will have learned to be a queen by watching her royal mother. That's how it works."

"But!" protested Lucy.

"I'm sure your mother taught you many wonderful things, but she wasn't a queen, now, was she?"

Lucy looked at her feet and mumbled angrily, "I wouldn't know what she was. Nobody tells me anything." She looked up. "But I'm a quick learner. And if I were his princess, Wynston wouldn't have to miss the blackberry patch on Sundays. It only makes sense."

At this the king laughed loudly, with a snort. "Oh, Lucy, you're such a child. You have to understand that there are ancient rules regarding these royal concerns. You can't be a princess simply because you and Wynston get along, or because you want to go berry picking, or because you'd enjoy each other's company, have pleasant lives, and rule the kingdom wisely and happily. *Suitable* isn't about pleasant or happy or fun. *Suitable* takes years of heavy learning and generations of careful breeding. And anyway, there's a law."

"A law?" Lucy asked. "A law against me?"

"Not exactly," answered the king. "Not a law against you as a person. Just a law against you ever, ever, ever living in this castle." Then he struck an odd pose, planted one hand on his velveted hip, pointed the index finger of his other hand in the air, and recited carefully: "By royal decree during the reign of Osbaldo the Humble, thirty-first king of Thistle, in the year of the great winds: *Only true nobility may reside within the gracious walls of the House of Thistle. So are the walls preserved.*"

Then he lowered his hand and turned to look at Lucy. "And you, I'm afraid, are just not noble, and therefore not a suitable match for Wynston. Nope. There's nothing we can do about it. You're common, my dear, no matter how sweet you happen to be."

Lucy didn't have a response for that.

"So you see, it will be a long while before Wynston can go for a walk with you. And once he's found his princess, he'll be occupied with murmuring sweet nothings and helping his lady wind her wool. Maybe you'd do well to find a new best friend. Besides, you and Wynston argue a great deal, anyway, don't you?" The king shook his head.

Lucy slipped down from the big chair and faced the king with her hands on her hips. "Well, even if he is busy finding a stupid princess, that's no excuse for missing an appointment in the berry patch. That's terribly rude!"

"Perhaps, but in any case, I've got to do something about this gravy." The king licked his shirt and whispered to himself, "Most definitely prickly-prune gravy—whatever was I thinking?"

Lucy left the hall and found her way out into the sunlight. She had a lump in her throat, but no idea why it was there. Why did it matter so much that Wynston had forgotten her this once? She forgot things all the time. She told herself there'd always be next weekend, or the weekend after that. But for the first time, she couldn't be certain about Wynston. And if she couldn't be certain of Wynston, what could she be sure of?

Lucy felt confused. She didn't know whether to be

angry or sad, and she didn't like either option. They seemed equally icky.

She walked home, kicking a pebble and muttering, "Suitable . . . shmootable . . . flootable." She thought, *I wonder what my mother would have to say about that!*

After a little ways, Lucy came to one of the pastures where her father led his cattle to graze. She stopped to scratch Verbena, the oldest and gentlest cow in the herd, on the nose with a stick. "Hey, Verbena . . . here, girl."

Verbena ambled over, followed by her daughter, Rosebud, a wily red animal. Rosebud herself had given birth to her first calf that spring, but the poor little thing had died only moments after. Ever since then, the young cow had been a bit funny in the head and more than a little wild, which endeared her to Lucy but no one else. As Verbena neared the fence, Rosebud split off and sprinted over to bury her nose in a gopher hole. Verbena *mooooo*ed loudly at her daughter, but Rosebud paid no mind. Verbena mooed again, and just then, Rosebud yelped as much as a cow can yelp—*"Mooo-yelp!"*—and pulled her nose fast out of the gopher hole. It was clear she'd gotten a nip.

"See, you should listen to Verbena," lectured Lucy. "You're lucky to have a good mama cow to teach you things. And don't you forget it!" She gave Verbena an affectionate scratch and a sympathetic gaze before she turned and continued on her way home.

When Lucy got back to the dairy, Sally was making soup and grumbling. She seemed more than a little angry at Lucy for deserting her on the way to market, so Lucy apologized and helped her chop the carrots and the celery. She rolled out fat noodles and minced garlic, and then she stood over the pot, stirring the soup and thinking more quietly than usual.

Then suddenly, for the second time in as many days, she felt two tears making their way down her cheeks. But this time she couldn't stop them. She made absolutely certain-sure that nobody saw her crying, but nevertheless, her tears fell into the good thick stew, so that her father complained that night, "More care with the salt next time. This tastes like it was made from seawater."

Sally said nothing, but Lucy wriggled uncomfortably in her chair at dinner. *What is wrong with me?* she wondered as she mopped up the salty soup with a hunk of brown bread. *I never used to cry like this. Never! Only ninnies cry.*

But none of this really helped matters. She still felt a little sad.

BEYOND THE VILLAGE

WHEN LUCY woke up the next day, she felt dreadful. She still couldn't decide whether to miss Wynston or to be angry with him. To cheer herself up, she crawled under the quilt and quietly sang her favorite song to her kitten, Mr. Boots.

Though winter snows may freeze us,
and spring storms flood our beds,
We're glad to feel the mountain grass
is pillowing our heads.
Though goats may be our closest friends,
and life is simple here,
We like it on the mountain,
where the air is sharp and clear.

Lucy paused between verses and wondered what it would be like to live on the mountain and run with the goats. She knew her mother had come from the mountain, where she'd learned the goatherd song. But that was all Lucy could remember. Lucy's head got all tangled up whenever she thought about her mother, which seemed to be more and more often lately.

Just a few weeks back she'd nervously asked Mrs. Peach, who sold ribbons in the square and knew absolutely everybody, about her mother. Mrs. Peach had said, "Oh, my sweet, there are things it's just best not to speak of. Your poor, poor father. I never saw a man so broken."

Then Mrs. Peach had shaken her head, handed Lucy a purple ribbon covered in yellow lace, and gone back to calling out, "Ribbons! Ribbons for sale! Get your nice fresh hot ribbons!" And while Lucy was of course pleased to have the ribbon, she still knew nothing about her mother.

But that was the day she'd started thinking. About secrets. About mysteries. About why someone might say *Hush!* And that was the day she'd realized that nobody, *nobody*, had actually ever said that her mother was dead. Why, she'd never even seen a grave for her mother down in the Thistle Cemetery, even though she'd spent a good deal of time there playing hide-and-seek. She'd probably read every single gravestone in the place, waiting for Wynston to pounce on her from the shadows, but she'd never seen her mother's name.

Slowly Lucy had begun to question: If her mother was alive, where had she gone? Why had she gone? The question was like a tiny little fly, buzzing around her head all the time. When she was busy, she barely noticed it, but when she was alone and the world got quiet, the fly seemed as loud as anything.

Lucy closed her eyes now and tried to picture the goats and her mother. In her mind the goats were white and her mother was a girl her own age. Then Lucy thought about what the king had said, about how a princess would learn to be a queen by watching her mother. But Lucy didn't even know exactly where her mother had come from. Maybe her mother had secretly been a queen. It wasn't likely, but anything was possible. . . . Maybe her mother was a laundress somewhere, or a baker. . . . Lucy would be fine with either of those. Just fine. It didn't matter what her mother did. Not a bit.

Then Mr. Boots made a throaty noise, and Lucy opened her eyes to look at him. He stretched one gray paw out and touched Lucy's nose. She began to sing again:

We have no use for fancy things,
  so keep your lace and jams.
We have no need for company,
  just labor for our hands.
And goats to sleep beside us,
  and bread to keep us full.
And stars above to guide us,
  and blankets made of wool.

Lying in her bed, with Mr. Boots purring and periodically nipping her fingers, Lucy thought and thought. Why was her mother such a mystery? Death was sad and hard, but it happened all the time. Wynston's mother had died, and that was no secret. Everyone talked about the horrible day when Queen Germantrude went boating, fell overboard, and was swallowed by a giant clam. It was certainly awful, but that didn't make it a *mystery.*

Perhaps Lucy's mother had done something bad, and then had to flee. Perhaps she had run away, back up the mountain—to labor with her hands and live by the stars, like the song said. And perhaps the reason Lucy's father never spoke about it was that he was ashamed of the awful thing Lucy's mother had done. Shame was a nasty feeling, Lucy knew. She thought about how Sally had wet her bed one night, dreaming of giant oceans made of apple juice. She'd been terribly embarrassed and had sworn Lucy to total secrecy. Lucy had never told, but even so, she knew Sally felt awful about it.

What did Lucy know about her mother? She knew that her mother's name had been Nora, because once in a while a neighbor twittered, "Oh, Nora would be so proud of the girls!" or "What would Nora have to say about that?" Each time it happened, Lucy's father stared silently at his feet. Which meant he was very sad and everyone else should be quiet.

She didn't exactly *miss* her mother because she couldn't exactly *remember* her mother, despite what she'd said to Sally . . . but there was something like an empty space in her belly when she thought the word *Mama*. She wondered—if her mother was alive—what she looked like, if her hair was brown or black or blond or purple or green or red, like Lucy's own. Had she grown fat? Or had, perhaps, the mountain life kept her young? Lucy imagined it was hard work, running with the goats. She finished the song.

We think of you with kindly thoughts,
  but seek the simple life.
We choose the mountain over
  all the joys of hearth and wife.
We've felt the sun from heaven,
  and breathed the mountain air
And now it seems that city life
  is too much life to bear.

Lucy had never thought about the last verse before, really thought about it. She'd never considered what might be hard to bear. But yesterday, between the king's mention of her mother and the loss of Wynston, Lucy had felt *burdened* for the first time herself. Or at least fumble-headed. Life seemed more complicated than she could remember, and she wasn't sure what she could do to make it simpler. She thought. And thought. And thought.

And the more she thought, the more convinced she became that she too belonged on the mountain with the goats. She wanted to see the guiding stars too. And most of all, she wanted to find her mother, figure out who she was and where she came from.

Mr. Boots meowed a tiny question at her, and Lucy

stroked his head. "I wouldn't stay away long, Mr. Boots. My home is here in Thistle. But maybe I could find out something about my mother. Maybe I have cousins on the mountain, or a grandmother, even!" In reply, Mr. Boots just yawned and stretched his claws into the heavy quilt.

"And maybe, just maybe, if I find her, I could bring her home . . . to Papa." Lucy whispered this to the kitten.

But Mr. Boots didn't have a thing to say about the matter. He pounced down onto the floor and exited the room. Lucy took in a gulp of air. She felt a nervous jittery stretchy feeling replace the ache in her belly.

All these years cloaked in quiet it had never occurred to her to take matters into her own hands. She pondered this and realized that she'd leaned too much on Wynston. Always waiting for Wynston, who was, she admitted to herself, a slowpoke. Lucy felt a tremor run down her spine as she imagined the mountain. *I can do this,* she thought. *I can find Mama, and I can do it by myself. I'll show all of them!*

Lucy followed Mr. Boots's example and climbed down herself, spurred by the jittery-belly feeling. She began to root around in the wooden trunk at the foot of her bed and finally emerged with a large cloth bag. She put her knitting into the bag, because without books to read or anyone to talk to, she knew she'd get terribly bored. A second later she put in a few extra skeins of yarn. After all, there was no telling how long she'd be gone. Maybe she could get her father's birthday slippers finished.

As she packed she thought about Wynston, tried to picture him with a roomful of princesses, and laughed a hard little laugh. *It's too bad*, she thought, *that Wynston has to be a king. It's so nice to be a blacksmith, or a carpenter. But there he is, stuck in that dusty castle, waiting to get all married and old. Still, that doesn't mean I can't have an adventure. . . . After all, it's not like I need his help.*

Lucy ate a good breakfast of warm ginger muffins and honey, with tea. Then she threw some apples and a loaf of bread into the bag with the knitting, in case she needed a snack to keep her going until she found a place to stay for the night. Finally, she wrapped her tin cup in a blanket and tossed the bundle into her bag.

She wrote a note for Sally and pinned it to the front door. On her way past the dairy, she noticed that Verbena was having trouble with Rosebud again. Each time Verbena nudged Rosebud over to where the best purple clover grew by the fence, Rosebud would let out a defiant *moo*. Then she'd scamper (as much as a cow can scamper) away. From a short distance, she'd peel bark from the fence post, chew it, and then spit it out, making a nasty face in the process. Lucy stopped to watch, and after Verbena's third attempt to nudge her daughter toward the most delicious food in the pasture, Lucy found herself unreasonably angry at the young cow.

"Do what your mother tells you, Rosebud!"

Rosebud stared at Lucy and then flicked her tail, as though to say, *I don't have to listen to her or to you either. Hmph!*

Verbena turned her head and gave Lucy a long stare. Lucy almost felt Verbena was asking for her help. So over the fence she went, leaving her bundle on the other side. She tumbled into the pasture, where she pulled a handful of clover and held it out to Rosebud.

But the cow curled her lip and turned her head away.

"Ooooh, Rosebud! Do you know how lucky you are to have a mother who loves you?" Lucy asked. "You're the most ungrateful little cow in the world. Here Verbena is, trying to give you the tastiest treat, and you're eating dried-out fence post instead."

Verbena bellowed in agreement.

"Somebody should teach you a lesson. If you only knew what it'd be like without your mother."

Rosebud stamped a foot, as if to say, *I'd be fine.*

"Oh, really?" asked Lucy. "You think so?" And with that she pulled a lead rope from the gate, tossed it around Rosebud's neck, and tightened the loop. "We'll see if you feel that way in a few days."

Verbena looked alarmed, but Rosebud threw Lucy a saucy glance and walked as far from Lucy as the lead rope would allow, back toward the fence post. She peeled off another piece of bark.

"Okay then," said Lucy. She opened the gate and led Rosebud out into the road. "Don't worry, Verbena," she said in a soothing voice. "I'll bring her back safe and sound. I can handle it."

Verbena did not seem entirely convinced.

But Lucy shouldered her bag, gripped Rosebud's rope tightly, and skipped on down the path. As she passed the castle, she waved cheerfully, out of habit, but only for a minute. Then she turned her head forward and walked on, whistling and humming. She wandered along and nodded goodbye to all the familiar houses and shops before leaving the village behind.

As she walked through the gates of Thistle, she felt

a tremor in her shoulders. A few hours of walking brought her into fields she'd never seen before, and she felt a rush of excitement. After about an hour of tramping along in unknown territory, she walked through a stand of trees and into the valley of the Scratchy Mountains, and her heart began to beat quickly. Her feet scurried along, trying to keep up with the pounding of her heart. She tugged on the cow to hurry.

"C'mon, Rosebud."

"Moo?"

Meanwhile, back at the castle, Wynston was throwing a little temper tantrum—an uncharacteristic fit—that Lucy would have been proud of. "Oh, Dad. Can't we stop for the day? I don't know any of this stuff . . . ," he whined at his father, who crouched before him in the most awkward curtsy imaginable.

"Come now, boy! You know we can't quit until you get this right." The king dipped his knees again. This time he made a ridiculous face, pushing out his lips and batting his eyelashes. He fluttered his hands and squealed improbably, "My beloved Prince Wynston, I have come from realms afar to join thee in thy royal cause. What wouldst thou have me do, to prove that I am a noble woman and worthy of thy gentle love and stately house?"

Wynston rolled his eyes, but he drew himself up and spoke as deeply as he could. "Fair lady, if you would only be—"

"No, no, and no, Wynston!" The king broke his pose and sighed. "She isn't a lady yet, son. Technically, she's still a maiden, so you have to call her *fair maiden*. Get it? Your aunt Lavinia thinks you're clever, but I'm beginning to wonder."

"Lady—maiden . . ." Wynston looked a smidge huffy, and mightily tired. "Does it really matter so much what I call her?"

"I can't believe I'm hearing this from you, boy!"

"It's just that nobody else has to do this sort of stuff, Dad. It doesn't make sense!"

King Desmond bellowed and pulled on his beard. "Wynston, what's come over you? You're usually such a good prince, so well behaved when it comes to these things."

"Well, Lucy says . . ."

"Ahhhh, I see. That Lucy. She's a lovely girl in so many ways, but she can certainly give a man a headache with all her questions. Not a suitable influence at all."

"But . . ."

"And what is this—this ridiculous preoccupation with making sense? I don't know what you youngsters are thinking half the time. It isn't *about* sense. It's *about* the rules. *The rules!*"

"Seriously, Dad, it isn't just Lucy that's making me think this. . . ."

"It isn't?"

"No, it's more than that. It's the whole idea of . . . this Queening stuff. I mean, why should some dumb princess have to prove anything to me? Who am I?" Wynston sat down on the floor, his face in his hands.

The king sighed and plopped down awkwardly beside his son. "Who are you? You're the prince of the realm, the heir apparent, the shining hope of your people, that's who you are. You are also a gigantic pain in my royal neck, to be honest. But this is not negotiable. Oh, if only your mother were here, maybe she could talk some sense into you."

"Well, how come nobody else has to follow the stupid rules? Why did I get stuck with all the guidelines?"

"Everyone has rules to follow, Wynston. It's just that not everyone has their rules written down for them on parchment."

Wynston had begun to listen, despite himself. He always had a hard time staying cranky at his father. "Like what kind of rules?"

"Well, take Tom the baker for example. He has lots of rules to follow, but instead of calling them rules he calls them recipes. What if he stopped adding eggs to the doughnuts one morning? You'd go in for a treat and the doughnuts would be all hard and stale like. You'd ask what the matter was, and Tom would say, 'Oh, you liked the eggy doughnuts? They were just an old-fashioned tradition. No special reason a doughnut has to have eggs in it.' And there you'd be with sugar all over your face and a rock in your gut, just because old Tom abandoned his rules. Just because he decided to try things a new-fangled way."

"Don't be silly," said Wynston. "It isn't the same at all."

"Isn't it?" The king raised an eyebrow.

Wynston made a funny face. "Of course not. First of all, Tom would never do that, because his rules make sense. And secondly, the princess Halcyon is not a doughnut, and thirdly, I don't care if she is, and fourthly—Omigosh—Dad!" Wynston clapped a hand to his mouth and jumped up to stare dramatically through the diamond-shaped window set into the stone wall across the room. "Oh *no!*"

"What? What? What?" the startled king stammered, louder with each breath.

"Gosh, Dad—there's a gigantic bird in your prize rosebush!" Wynston, wide-eyed, pointed a finger toward the gardens. "I think it might even be a vulture or something. Wow, it's HUGE!"

"What bird? Where?" King Desmond scrambled off the floor and flew to the window, but as he turned his royal back, Wynston bolted for the door. He ran down to the kitchen and escaped from the castle, free for the first time all week. He wasn't quite sure why he'd done it. Too many rules, maybe—an overdose of etiquette. He had just needed to get *out*! And now, he was.

As he raced across the lawn, he felt his heart pounding up through his rib cage, and it wasn't just because he was running hard, though he was. His heart was beating fast because, for the first time, he had thoroughly defied his father. He'd never done something so . . . bad . . . before in his life, and he was at once excited and frightened. Lucy would be proud.

Lucy! He had to see Lucy. He felt awful about missing their weekly berrying excursion, but just wait until she heard about this!

"...there's a gigantic bird in your prize rosebush!"

When he got to Lucy's house, Wynston found Sally on the front porch in tears, her head buried in her apron. But Lucy was nowhere to be seen. He tapped Sally's knee gently. "What's wrong? Did the dogs get into the smokehouse again?" Sally blew her nose and kept crying.

Wynston wasn't surprised by this, since Sally was notoriously weepy. He tried again. "There's a fair coming to town next week— Hey, that's a lovely dress, Sal— Want a licorice button?" Wynston pulled a rather grubby piece of candy from his pocket and put it on Sally's knee, but Sally continued with her rainstorm.

Wynston leaned back on the steps and sighed. He waited, hummed, chewed a piece of onion grass—until one little hand crept from under the apron. In it was a note, very damp and a little torn. Wynston took the drippy note, and this is what it said:

Dear Sally,

Please don't mind too much, but I'm off to see the Scratchy Mountains—you know, where Mother came from. I want to climb clear to the top! And if all goes well, I'll have a big, big surprise for you (and Papa!) when I get home. I know you'll help

with my share of the milking, and I'll bring you a
nice present, I promise. I left a lemon cake in the
bread box for dinner, and I love you very much.

> *Your sister,*
> *Lucy*

Wynston read the note four times before he looked up. "How could she leave without me?" He scratched his head. "I would've gone too."

Sally mopped her face with her sleeve and tucked a strand of hair behind her ears. She sniffed. "I'm sure I don't know, but it means I've got to do all the milking and cooking. Plus carry all the firewood by myself. And now . . . as if things aren't bad enough, one of our cows has gone missing. What an awful day." She went back to crying, but mumbled into her skirts, "Did she tell you how long she'd be gone?"

"I swear, I didn't know she was planning this at all. I haven't seen her all week."

"But she went to the castle yesterday to see you, didn't she?" Sally stopped crying and looked at Wynston.

"What makes you think that?" asked Wynston. "Yesterday I got fitted for a new pair of beaded boots, learned to eat fish soup with a tiny fork, and studied the ancient art of holding my tongue without getting it wet. I was pretty busy, but I think I'd have known if Lucy stopped by."

"Maybe," said Sally. "All I know is that she ran off to the castle yesterday and left me to carry everything home from the market. And it was potato day too!"

Wynston bit his thumbnail. "And you haven't seen her since?"

"Only at supper—" Sally said. But Wynston was halfway across the yard before she could finish her thought. So Sally went inside, to weep and sweep. When she was finished, she leaned her cheek against the broom handle and rubbed away her last tear. *There!* Tidying up always made Sally feel better.

Back at the castle, Wynston slipped in through the kitchen door and bumped into Masha, who was tossing flour around the pantry with wild abandon. "Well, if it isn't the prince! Answer me this, Wynston, and tell me the honest truth—no need to soften the blow. Do you think a pear tart counts as a pie? Truly?" Masha looked very worried, but Wynston was in a hurry.

"I'm sure it does," he said, heading straight for the stairs.

She breathed deeply and forced a smile. "Oh, good. Then that makes fourteen pies altogether, and I can save Miss Lucy's berries to go with the custard."

Wynston turned. "Lucy's berries?"

"Oh, Miss Lucy brought by some fresh blackberries— an entire milk-pailful. I'm blushing to think I begged for 'em, but I was in such a whizzle-tiz when she stopped in on Sunday. She's a sweet girl, Miss Lucy is. Generous."

"What'd she want?"

"She asked could you come out to play, and I told her you was frightful busy, with all the castle goings-on. Then she went along to the berry patch."

Wynston touched a finger to the pear tart softly. "So then, she stopped in yesterday to bring the berries?"

"No, love. She left 'em for me Sunday night on her way home. Yesterday she came and saw your father."

Wynston studied the cook carefully. "Lucy came to see my father?"

"Yes indeedy, but she wasn't here long. I only saw her through the window, on my way upstairs to feed the parrots. She was knocking on the front door, all formal-like."

"The front door? That doesn't sound like Lucy."

"She looked a little sad, now that I think of it."

"Sad."

"Yes, well, sad, a bit. Or maybe not. I don't know. As I said, I only saw her from a distance."

"Lucy was sad?"

"At any rate, she just went on home, so it must not've been too important. Now, love, I need to be getting to my biscuits, or we'll never have dinner." When Masha turned and reached into the icebox for a giant jug of buttermilk, Wynston snuck back out the door. He headed into the yard and then perched on the gate to think, just exactly as Lucy had done two days before.

Lucy, all alone on the mountain! That didn't seem right. She could be headstrong, loud, bossy, and stubborn, but Lucy did *not* like to be alone. She was a ringleader—his ringleader—and everybody knows that a ringleader needs a ring. He scratched his head and wondered what had made her run off.

He wondered, *Why the mountains?* Wynston couldn't help being worried.

CAT THE DOG AND
WILLIE WIMPLE

LUCY AND Rosebud walked all day toward the Scratchy Mountains, and for a while, everything looked like the soft fields near Thistle. But as the mountains grew closer and taller above her, Lucy began to feel a nervous tug. She looked up, searching for the singing goatherds. But she didn't see anyone at all, and she felt very very tiny beneath the enormous mountains. She stopped to drink beside a river and noticed that the fish nibbling at her ankles were blue, not like the silver fish in Thistle Creek. When she crossed a small road cutting through the valley, she discovered that the pebbles in the road were black, instead of the pale sand color of all proper pebbles at home. Lucy gathered a few of the odd stones for Sally.

Just as the sun was getting ready to set, Lucy stopped outside a small wood. She'd come to the base of the mountains, and the trees before her were taller than anything she'd ever seen. They weren't the soft brown color of the dogwood trees near the dairy, or even the gray-blue-green of the sad willows beside the castle moat. These trees were covered in stiff needles that shed a dark shade over the entire wood, and they looked almost black in the fading light. A cold wind snaked by her, and Lucy reached out a hand to stroke Rosebud on the nose. She imagined that she could see small mean animals darting among the trees. She could almost hear their sharp teeth grinding and chomping. Rosebud's nose was a warm and snuffly comfort to Lucy's cold hand. Suddenly Lucy was exhausted.

"No harm in camping here for the night," called Lucy to the wood, loudly, in case anyone or *anything* was listening. "Rosebud needs to rest, and the grass is nice and soft." She tied Rosebud to the nearest tree trunk and spread out her blanket. She sat down to eat but instead fell directly asleep, apple in hand. Rosebud settled down beside her, and then, very suddenly, so did the sun. The sky turned a deep purple, veined with rivers of light, streaks of the palest orange imaginable. The Scratchy

Mountains towered black against the ocean of violet and gold, but only Rosebud noticed. She licked Lucy's cheek, but Lucy didn't stir.

Lucy woke to a bright morning and immediately tried to pull a pillow over her eyes. Since she had no pillow, she ended up tugging on a bit of Rosebud instead. The young cow let out a cry, and Lucy sat up fast. She rubbed her head and discovered that the valley looked altogether different from how it had at dusk.

The peaks above her were deeply green and lush, and a small river ran into the wood, bubbling cheerfully beneath a hum of waving cattails and darting dragonflies. She untied Rosebud, and the two of them scampered down to the river for a drink. Then Lucy washed her face and milked Rosebud onto the grass. (Every milk cow needs to be milked each morning, and Lucy—no matter that she might also be an adventurer—was a diligent milkmaid.) She drank a cup of milk while she was at it, and ate some bread while Rosebud grazed on a patch of good grass. Then she folded up her blanket and started into the wood.

Inside the wood, pine needles had been falling softly for years, and they made a thick carpet on the ground. Lucy trod lightly, rope in hand. The ground felt bouncy, like walking on her bed at home—if her bed were much,

much bigger and covered in trees. Lucy thought of Wynston. For a minute, she wanted to turn back and fetch him, so he could walk in the soft wood too. Then she remembered that she was angry, and she said to Rosebud, "Who needs a boy along? Someday, if he's lucky, I'll tell Wynston all about it, if he has the time to listen, but anyway—I'm glad he isn't here now."

Rosebud snorted, and Lucy answered tartly, "What?" Rosebud snorted again.

"Truly! I really *am* glad he isn't here!" Rosebud said nothing as the two walked on, deeper into the woods.

After an hour or so, the ground started to slope upward, and the walking became more difficult. The trees thinned out until the wood was gone, and Lucy and Rosebud found themselves scrambling over a bare incline rubbly with rocks and riddled with strange lumps the size of watermelons. Lucy stepped onto one of the lumps and then jumped to the next, which stood about two feet away. From there, she jumped to another little hillock, and then to another. She went quicker, more nimbly each time, until she was hopping at a furious pace. Rosebud, tired from walking, stopped to watch this odd behavior. She snorted indignantly.

"Hey, this is fun!" Lucy called out to Rosebud, but

the cow wasn't interested in the least. Instead she chewed a pale green plant she found sprouting from one of the tiny clumps of earth. But she looked up suddenly when Lucy cried out, "Oh!" Then she ambled over to where Lucy stood, to see what had caused the "Oh!"

Lucy was staring at a little creature curled up beside one of the tiny hills. In fact, the creature was hugging the hill, as though the hill were a person. Though the animal's eyes were shut and he seemed to be sleeping, he trembled.

"Maybe he's dreaming," Lucy whispered to Rosebud, who stared at the furry little body the size of a large cat.

Rosebud *moo*ed in response, which woke the creature. It looked up, startled, and hugged tighter to the hill.

Lucy knelt down to examine the creature. She was nervous that she might be bitten, but her curiosity was greater than her fear. "What are you?" she asked, "and where did you come from?"

The creature whimpered a little *"mrooooowr."* He scrabbled at his hill for comfort and dug at the ground, looking for a safe place to hide. Finding none, he finally fell away and rolled over onto his feet. Though he was cowering beside the hill, he looked up at Lucy.

Lucy had never seen a prairie dog before, so she didn't know what to call the beast. The prairie dog had never seen a Lucy before, and so he just stared, his nose shuddering now and then. Lucy thought he looked more frightened than anything else. She reached out her hand slowly. In a soft voice she said, "Are you all alone? Are you hungry?"

The creature stretched out his nose, as though to smell Lucy. She moved her hand an inch closer. And he licked it gently.

"Look, he likes me," Lucy said to Rosebud. She scratched the creature's little nose and he closed his eyes for a split second. He made a snuffling sound and Lucy smiled.

But then the creature stood up and barked, *"Owrf!"* And Lucy jumped. The creature ran quickly toward her. Without knowing what she was doing, Lucy screamed and ran to hide behind Rosebud as the sharp noise of the dog's chatter filled the air. *"Owrf-owrf! Owrf-owrf-owrf!"*

"What terrible sounds it's making!" said Lucy, clapping her hands over her ears. "I thought he was cute, but he's simply awful. No manners at all!"

Rosebud lost interest after about thirty seconds. She went back to chewing the pale green plant. "Maybe—do you think he bites?" asked Lucy from behind the cow's flank. Rosebud didn't even turn her head.

Finally the prairie dog stopped barking, and Lucy peeked out from behind the cow. But the small furry animal was nowhere to be seen. "I suppose there's nothing to be done," she said aloud. "Although he seemed so lonely, and truly I don't think he could have hurt me much—even if he had bitten me. As small as he was." Rosebud gave Lucy a doubtful glance.

"Well, he seemed so . . . lost. I wonder where he came from."

Though Lucy couldn't have known it, the creature had in fact run away from his own home—fled his safe little tunnel for the mountain—just as Lucy had fled Thistle the day before. But Rosebud didn't know that, and wasn't especially interested, if you want to know the truth. So Lucy continued.

"But if he's going to chatter and run like that, then perhaps you're right, Rosebud. Maybe he wouldn't be much fun to travel with. Still, I wouldn't have minded the extra company."

She picked up Rosebud's lead and was about to start walking again when she happened to glance over her shoulder. There sat the animal, who'd been following her in a slow circle around the cow, evading her notice. Now he was settled on the ground two feet behind Lucy, licking his paws.

He stopped licking and stared at her intently. "Oh,

there you are!" Lucy said. "C'mere," she whispered, "little man, little creature. I won't hurt you." The prairie dog scratched an ear and blinked. "I don't even know what you are." The animal inched a little closer and settled beside Lucy, so she bent to pet its small head. "But perhaps it doesn't matter."

Unfortunately, just as Lucy bent to touch him, the creature sneezed.

"Oh!" shouted Lucy, jumping.

The animal rubbed his wet nose against Lucy's leg and said, *"Owr-Mrththth?"*

"Oh, you poor sniffly beast," said Lucy. "Do you have a home?"

He just looked at her pleadingly and made his sound again. *"Owr-Mrththth?"*

"Maybe you'd do best to come along with us . . . since you seem to be travelling alone. Though I can't imagine what sorts of things you like to eat."

But when Lucy bent to pick him up, he scurried away.

"All right, I've had enough of this game. I'm leaving," she said, turning around. "But if you want to come, you're welcome to join us." She looked over her shoulder at him.

The animal stared pathetically. He wiped a paw across his little face and then barked decidedly. *"Owrooof-oof."*

Lucy and Rosebud began walking. After a few steps, Lucy glanced over her shoulder and saw the short furry beast scrambling over small hills and rocks, following at a steady pace. She smiled as she sang over her shoulder.

I'm pleased as punch to have you join
Our cheerful company.
Despite your sniffles, whistles, barks,
And doubtful pedigree.
If only I could speak your tongue,
Then I might ascertain
What kind of sniffly barky word
Would make a fitting name.

Mile upon mile, as Lucy walked, the creature followed, scrambling behind. But when she came to a little bridge over a fast-moving river, the creature appeared at Lucy's foot, kneading its little paws and rubbing its face. Then the animal nudged Lucy's foot with his nose and sneezed twice. *"Fishtoo! Fishtoo!"* His eyes were sleepy, and he was too cute to ignore.

"All right!" said Lucy. "I guess I don't mind carrying you a ways. But then you'll really have to have a name. I suppose you're almost a cat. Cat? Are you a cat?"

Cat said nothing in response.

"Maybe you don't know what you are either. But I don't suppose it matters."

And that is how Cat the prairie dog followed Rosebud the cow and Lucy the girl onto the first stretch of the first peak of the mountain range known as the Scratchy Mountains. They walked all day over the rocky terrain, stopping now and then to pick pebbles from their feet or to stare at the odd orange wildflowers that snapped shut when Lucy touched them. By dinnertime they could see something dark far off in the distance. There appeared to be a low gray cloud hung like a ring around the mountain.

"If it's raining on the mountain, we'll want to wait until tomorrow to pass by," said Lucy. So they made camp, curling up together in a scooped-out place in the earth where a few smooth boulders formed a windbreak. Lucy was hungry, and finished off her bread. She offered an apple to Rosebud, who gratefully munched it from her hand. Then she gave one to Cat, who only wrapped his short furry arms around the piece of fruit. Hugging the apple like a friend, Cat curled up and began to breathe heavily, with a whistle. Lucy pulled her blanket close around her shoulders and thought, *If only I had a picture of this night—me, alone on the mountain. When I find my mother, she'll be so proud.* Then she drifted off to sleep.

In the middle of the night, Lucy woke up to find herself freezing, even though she was wedged between the warm bodies of Cat and Rosebud. She turned over quietly and wrapped her arms tightly around her middle, but still she was cold. She thought of her warm bed at home, of the fire in the kitchen. She tried not to think about Wynston in his castle. She whispered into the cold night air, "I do wish it was just a little warmer here."

Then Rosebud shifted and lowed deeply. Cat gave an odd shudder and wrapped his arms around Lucy's neck. He snuggled against her, and suddenly Lucy was warmer. Much.

Poor Wynston felt very bad as he sat on the gate, in that muddle-headed way you feel when your parents leave you in charge of the house and you forget to do something very important, and then you realize you've forgotten to do something, but you don't know what the something is. If you just sit, you usually imagine that the basement is filling with water or the roast is burning or the dog is running away.

Wynston kicked his feet and felt a lot like that. He wasn't even sure where Lucy had gone, but he couldn't believe she hadn't waited for him. At the same time, he thought deep down that maybe Lucy was angry, or sad, or lonely, or that she didn't want to be his friend anymore (getting left behind can make you think strange thoughts). He knew his father might be able to explain things a little, since he had spoken with Lucy, but Wynston wanted to give his royal father a while to cool down, after the rose-bush prank. Wynston was surprised he didn't feel more horrible about the prank, but maybe it was just because he felt so bad about Lucy. All the badness was getting tangled up inside of him.

See? thought Wynston. *This is why it's best to stay out of trouble!*

Wynston felt *a mess*. And the worst thing to do when you feel *a mess* is to *sit still*, and the best thing to do is to *do something*, so Wynston did. He hopped down from the gate, raced to the royal stables, and saddled his horse, Sprout (which is not a very good name for a royal steed but is a perfect name for a sweet, spotted horse). Then Wynston rode away, tearing across the fields in no particular direction, just as you might if you tried to *do something* when you weren't quite sure what to do.

Wynston jumped some hedgerows and splashed in a river and tore through a glen and galloped and galloped and galloped. He raced around until both he and Sprout were out of breath and a little lost. Then they stopped at a creek for a drink, and Wynston noticed something very serious. He discovered his crown was missing, but had no idea where on his wild ride he'd lost it.

Oddly, even though he knew he'd be in trouble when he got home, Wynston felt just fine—better, actually. Instead of feeling frightened of what his father would say, Wynston felt light as a bird. It felt nice not to be wearing that heavy metal band. In any case, he couldn't fix any of it this minute, so what was the use in fretting?

"Well, I guess I'm just not a prince today!" he said to nobody in particular. "I guess I'm just me." He felt much better than he had felt sitting on the gate, but he was hungry. He looked in his pockets, but there was only the squashed licorice button. He nibbled at it and felt even hungrier.

So he walked, holding Sprout's reins, until he found a dirt road. He followed the dirt road until he found a little round house that looked like an apple, with a chimney for a stem. Wynston knocked on the door of the little round house, through which he could hear strange muffled sounds. But nobody answered.

So he knocked more than a few times, and then he stood listening to the muffled sounds and trying to decide whether to open the door. He knew it was a cardinal rule of etiquette never to enter a strange house uninvited. But Wynston was beginning, for the first time in his twelve long princely years, to question the rules of etiquette. Besides, the muffled sounds worried him. Finally, when the noise of his growling belly had gotten loud enough to drown out the muffled sounds, Wynston tied Sprout to the gatepost. He pushed the door open and peered inside nervously, but then began to laugh. He couldn't help it.

There before his eyes was a very round bottom—an enormous round bottom in a pair of yellow britches. The bottom was wedged tightly into a huge stew pot sitting on the large fireplace at the center of the room. The legs connected to the bottom wiggled furiously. The head and arms connected to it were, of course, hidden inside the pot. No matter how the legs wiggled and the feet kicked, the bottom would not budge. The fireplace, thank goodness, was cold.

Once he'd stopped laughing, Wynston flew to the rescue of the large round bottom in the yellow britches. You might wonder how Wynston knew what to do in such a sticky situation. But if you've ever eaten a jar of

The bottom was wedged tightly into a huge stew pot . . .

gooseberry jam with your fingers (which Wynston had done, at Lucy's urging) and then gotten your jammy fist stuck tightly in the jam jar (which Wynston had also done), then you know the answer.

Wynston walked to the butter churn, reached in, and pulled out a lump of greasy yellow butter. Then he went back to the pot and began to squish the butter around the bottom in the yellow britches. He walked slowly around the pot until he'd painted a huge greasy ring between the rim of the pot and the britches.

Of course, this tickled the bottom so that whoever was inside the pot began to giggle, then to guffaw. But the wiggling and the giggling and the butter worked, and suddenly, there was a loud thump! Wynston found himself looking at the upper end of the bottom in the yellow britches. "Most thankful," gasped a very red face. "I'm most thankful for your help. Been in there all day. If there's anything I can do to repay you, I'm happy to oblige."

Wynston laughed and licked his buttery hand. "Well, I'd love to hear the story of how you got stuck in the soup pot, but first, perhaps lunch. Do you think I might have a little lunch? I'm starving." As if to prove him right, his belly let out a particularly curious noise.

"Certainly," said the man with the enormous bottom,

politely pretending not to notice the curious belly noise. "I wouldn't mind a bit of lunch myself, seeing as I spent the breakfast hour inside a soup pot. But first, proper introductions. I'm Willie." He stuck out a chubby hand for shaking.

"And I'm Wynston." Wynston shook as well as he could with his slidy buttery hand.

Willie's eyes widened. "Prince Wynston? Desmond's tyke? King-to-be?"

"Among other things," said Wynston, looking uncomfortable. His hand moved to his head, groping for his missing crown.

Willie was that rare sort of grown-up who knows when to stop talking. He didn't ask any more questions, but instead piled the table with bread and mustard, cold chicken, and rice pudding. He poured two big glasses of milk and then sat down to eat. Wynston ate faster, but Willie ate more, and when they were finished, Willie pushed back his chair and loosened his belt. "So, are you on an adventure? A quest? A voyage? I love fascinating stories after lunch."

Wynston shook his head. "Sorry. No adventure. I guess I'm just riding my horse around. It sounds kind of dumb when I say it out loud like that. . . ."

"No need to apologize at all. I think that's a fine thing. A fine thing. Not enough people just ride around these days. Everyone's always *getting somewhere.* And once they get where they're going they just need to go somewhere else. It's silly, really. Much better to just ride around."

Wynston was surprised. "I hadn't thought about it like that."

Willie nodded. "Yessirree. Just riding around. See what you find when you get there. That's a good boy."

"Thank you, I think," said Wynston. "Though my father might not agree."

But Willie tactfully ignored Wynston's mention of the king. "Which way are you going anyway? West? Or maybe you're heading for something in-betweenish. Say, east-southerly . . ."

It was a simple question, but a good one, since Wynston didn't know the answer. Still, he wasn't surprised when he heard himself answer nervously, "I don't know. I thought I might be going *up.*"

"Up?"

"Up, like, to see the Scratchy Mountains. I have a friend there, I hope."

"Ah—the Scratchy Mountains!" laughed Willie. "Can't say that I blame you. I'm from those parts myself, and I still

miss the sunrise over the Blue Forest every blessed morning. But I wouldn't suggest you stay there long. A few days
in the Scratchy Mountains will be plenty."

"Why's that?"

"Oh, no particularly particular reason. It's just a long
way up."

"Well, can you tell me how to start?"

"Surely I can. It's a snap. Just follow this road through
those trees there, and then follow the river. That'll get you
to the base of the first mountain, and then you'll start
climbing. Try to keep the river in sight and you can't get
too lost."

Wynston felt a little confused at how quickly the
adventure was taking hold of him, but he was pleased to
have a plan. So he thanked his new friend, wiped his
mouth, and went outside to check on Sprout. When
Willie came to the door to say goodbye, he was holding a
bundle of food in one hand and a letter in the other.
"You've been more than helpful already, what with that
embarrassing soup-pot situation. But do you think you
could do me one more favor?"

Wynston nodded as he climbed onto Sprout. "Of
course."

"If you happen to pass through the town at the top

of the first mountain—called Torrent—get this letter to my mother, Persimmon Wimple. I haven't been home in years, and it's awful hard to get mail up the mountain. The folks in Torrent aren't much for mingling, and so there's no regular postal service."

"Sure thing," said Wynston, happy to help. "Maybe you'll do me a favor too?"

"Anything!" said Willie. "What can I do?"

"Just don't . . . tell anyone where I've gone."

"I wouldn't dream of it," said Willie. "I was a boy once too, you know."

Wynston smiled a little, imagining bumbling Willie as a boy. He put the letter in his pocket and tied the bundle onto his back. As Sprout began to move, he said, laughing, "Someday I still want to hear the story of how you got into the soup pot."

"Oh, the usual way!" Willie answered jovially.

Wynston couldn't help laughing out loud.

"Do be careful!" called Willie, as an afterthought.

But Wynston was already moving at a gallop, and he heard only the wind rushing past.

THE SHORT CUT, THE LONG CUT, AND THE CURIOUS STORM

LUCY WOKE up terribly hungry, and she ate an apple while Rosebud tried (with very little luck) to graze on the bare earth at the foot of the mountain. Then Lucy milked Rosebud, staring up-up-up at the summit. She noticed that the strange, heavy gray cloud was still there, but that the weather seemed otherwise fine. So she folded her blanket, dusted her skirts, and drank her milk. Then she roused Cat, who was no more interested in his breakfast milk than he had been in his apple, which Lucy now brushed off and tucked back into her bag. Lucy shook her finger at the creature. "I must say, Cat . . . I've never heard of a cat who doesn't like milk in the morning." But Cat had nothing to say in reply. He took off chasing a big black beetle, which he then munched in one giant bite. Lucy shuddered.

After that there was nothing left to do but climb, to leave the rocky rubble and the boulders and begin the steep journey up.

"Well," said Lucy, "I suppose this is what I came here for." She took a deep breath, walked to the nearest tree, and snapped off the smallest branch for a walking stick. Then she began to hike into the forest, with Rosebud following right behind her and Cat scrambling to keep up.

It was hard going at first, but then it got even harder. The ground was stony and rough, and the trees made the path dark. The mountain wasn't especially scary, but Lucy was lonely, the walking was dull, and the top of the mountain seemed very far away. From time to time, Lucy had to carry Cat, whose short, furry legs couldn't move very fast. She was beginning to doubt she'd ever reach the top, but she imagined her mother tossing her hair in the wind and calling to the goats, and a little burst of energy shot through her. Then—she couldn't help it—she thought of Wynston. To distract herself, Lucy made up a song.

When climbing up a mountain,
  be sure to bring your feet—
You'll need them to escape from
  hungry lions that you meet.
And if you make it past the beasts
  and thieves and angry bears—
However far the summit seems,
  it's twice as far as there.

But the song didn't help much and Lucy still felt lonely, so she tried talking to Rosebud. "What do you think Sally's making for supper tonight, girl?" But Rosebud was hungry and confused, and she just clomped along beside Lucy in a contrary way. Lucy sighed. Her adventure wasn't feeling very adventure-ish anymore. She walked and walked. Then she walked some more. The further she walked, the less interested she felt in the mountains.

Then she saw a goat. A little white shape, pale against the dark green of the mountain. And when she squinted her eyes against the sun, Lucy could just make out a person a few yards away from the goat. Lucy rubbed her eyes, but she couldn't tell at this great distance if the person was a girl or a boy, an old person or a child.

She called, "Helloooooooooooo!" and was surprised when the person waved at her. Faintly she could hear an echo, "Helloooooooooooo!" coming back at her through the air. A woman's voice, Lucy thought, though she couldn't be sure it wasn't just the echo of her own call.

She jumped up and down and yelled again, "Helllll-llooooooooooo!" The woman—if she was indeed a woman—waved back once more and said something, but her words bounced off the rock walls and became muffled and indistinct. After a few minutes, Lucy gave up all hope of communicating with the distant figure and moved on. She thought maybe she'd catch up to her if she walked fast enough. Lucy felt a nervousness building like hunger in her belly. She walked even faster. She was almost running, and it was all the others could do to keep up. But then she slowed her frenzied pace and began to ponder.

What if that was my mother? wondered Lucy. A few minutes later, *What if that was her, and she doesn't want to see me?* A little further along, Lucy stopped walking. *What if I was the burden she ran away from?* She stood still. But after a minute of thinking this terrible thought, she shrugged it off.

At what might have been lunchtime, they stopped to

rest along a particularly overgrown stretch of the mountain path. Lucy cleared away a pile of pine cones and sat down to eat, but there wasn't much lunch to be had. Just Cat's leftover apple, split between Lucy and Rosebud (Cat still wasn't interested). So Lucy wandered off the path to forage among the trees. She returned with a handful of dandelion greens and a pocket full of walnuts. While Rosebud nibbled at a patch of crabgrass and Cat disappeared behind a boulder to inspect (and perhaps ingest) a disgusting anthill, Lucy ate her sharp-tasting weeds with a cup of milk. She was still hungry, so she sat down in the dirt to crack the nuts. First she pounded on them with a rock, cutting her finger. Then she tried to smash a walnut with the heel of her boot, but the nut rolled beneath her foot and she toppled into a prickle bush.

Lucy lay there in the bush. She didn't cry, exactly, but she did grit her teeth and make a funny little exasperated sound. Then she sat up and rubbed her eyes. She stared at the cut on her finger and wished she were anywhere else. "Oh, FRAZZLE!" she said out loud. "I hate to admit it, but I miss Wynston. Why did I think I could do this alone?" Lucy sighed deeply. "I'm a silly."

But it was worse than that, bigger than that. Sitting like a lump in the nettles where she'd fallen, she felt a momentary shiver of real fear. Because she was alone, and no song was going to fix this.

Then a terrible thought occurred to her. *What's even worse is . . . the trouble this might cause. Because now I'm lost, for a no-good reason, and if I stay up on the mountain, someone else is sure to come looking for me. And then someone will have to go looking for them, and so on and so on. Oh, this was a mistake.* She lay back in the nettles, thinking hungrily.

After a while, Cat returned from behind the boulder, chewing happily on a large brown cricket. He crawled into the prickle bush with Lucy, curled up in her lap, and licked her hand.

Lucy felt a little better, and she sat up. "Oh, Cat, thank you. You know, I'm awfully glad to have found you."

Cat blinked twice. *"Owrf."*

"But no matter how nice you may be," said Lucy, "you can't help me with this. I worry I'm not the best mother a catlike beast could have. It seems I can barely take care of myself."

Lucy patted Cat's head and sighed. "I think you're a lovely creature, Cat. But right now I wish you were a person instead of a whatever-you-really-are. Then you might be able to tell me what to do."

Cat just licked his paws and rubbed his nose in a

very un-person-like manner, so Lucy clambered out of the prickles, pulled a few stray thorns from her stockings and hair, and said, "I give up."

Cat said, *"Owr-rowrff,"* and blinked harder than usual, which made Lucy a little defensive.

"Well, so what? I've thought about it a good deal. I'm not having much fun, and this walk will take us months at the rate we're going. Even if I do find Mama, she must not want to see me . . . or she'd have come home long ago, right? I'm worse than a silly . . . I'm a fool! So who else wants to go home?" Nobody responded, but it didn't matter. Lucy was ready to turn back.

But sometimes when you're trying to have an adventure, the adventure is also trying to have you. So the minute Lucy wanted to turn around and scurry back to Thistle, Cat wandered off. When Cat wandered off, Rosebud happened to step on a very sharp stone that cut her foot.

The cow let out a mournful, horrible, sad sound, the low of a young milk cow with an empty belly and a hurt foot.

"Oh!" said Lucy, running over to examine the poor foot, which was bleeding a little. She pulled the pointed pebble from where it had gotten stuck in the tender hoof, and then she wrapped the sore foot up in a big leaf and tied it with a piece of yarn from her unfinished knitting. Lucy felt bad bad bad. "Oh, I'm a beast. I had to go and run off and now we're lost and your foot is bleeding, so you can't walk on it today and maybe not even tomorrow. And we're all hungry and nobody even knows where we are. This is a terrible horrible disastrous disaster." Rosebud gave a snuffle and leaned her big soft head down to rest it on Lucy's neck. "I'm so sorry, girl," said Lucy. "I'll get you home, I promise."

Rosebud gave a second snuffle, and Lucy said, "No, really, I mean it. I'll get you back to Thistle. Somehow."

But just then they both started and jumped because Cat gave a shriek from the trees. *"Owr-owrrrrrrrrrf!"*

Lucy ran into the brush to find Cat shivering excitedly beside a small river. In the small river was a small boat, just big enough for a young milk cow, a girl, and a cat-size prairie dog. A fine fit.

Lucy felt her spirits lift as she thought back to the map in the throne room in Thistle. She remembered the rivers that ran up and down the sides of the mountain. "What luck!" she said. "We'll be home in no time now." She gathered up her few things and took Rosebud's lead.

But often when something appears too good to be true, that is precisely the case. Lucy was so excited about

the boat that she failed to notice something very important. Something very important! Just as the fish and the
rocks at the base of the mountain had been different
colors from the fish and the rocks in Thistle, and just as
the strange flowers seemed magical when they snapped
shut, so this river was strange. But it wasn't until Lucy
had settled Rosebud (with some difficulty) into the boat's
stern, seated Cat securely in the bow, untied the boat, set
it loose in the current, and hopped in—it wasn't until the
boat began to move that Lucy noticed just how strange
the river was. When she did, she exclaimed, "Oh my!"
But by then it was too late.

"Oh my gosh! Cat! Rosebud! This boat isn't taking
us back to Thistle at all. I don't know how, but this boat
is moving *up* the river."

And so it was. It moved quickly, zipping up the side
of the mountain, so that the trees and the bushes and the
animals in the forest were a blur to Lucy. Cat shook
gently, the fur on his little face blowing in the breeze.
Rosebud settled down to enjoy the smooth ride, content
not to walk any further on her wounded foot. And Lucy
worried a little, but not too much. After all, riding in the
boat was far preferable to walking all day, and she had to
admit the view was lovely. As she passed a little herd of

brownish goats and a sleeping goatherd, she laughed out loud. Whatever might be lurking at the mountaintop, her adventure had found her at last.

Now, if Lucy, Cat, and Rosebud had trudged along with their eyes glued to the top of the first Scratchy Mountain, they never would have found the little boat. But the adventure wanted them on the mountain, and so they wandered off the most obvious path and found themselves the shortest short cut of all. Wynston was not so lucky, if lucky is what they were.

Because he had a letter in his hand with "Persimmon Wimple, village of Torrent" written neatly at the top, Wynston plodded along in the direction he believed to be the village of Torrent, which was up. He followed the path and led Sprout along with great care. Wynston was nothing if not careful. Even if he'd just broken his father's rules for the first time in his life, he was determined to break the rules . . . carefully. It was in his nature.

He kept his eyes straight ahead. In the daytime, he rode in the saddle at a regular pace, trying to think of what he'd say when he saw Lucy. And when it got dark, he threw a saddle blanket over Sprout and slept beneath the makeshift tent it formed. He ate from the sack that Willie had filled for him, and he drank from the little stream beside the path. In fact, he barely noticed the things around him—the odd little beasts, the strange trees, and the radiant sunrises. He wanted only to get to the top of the mountain, to deliver his letter, to find Lucy, and to go home. It was dull riding, and he remembered almost nothing of the adventure when he got to Torrent.

When the boat carrying Lucy, Rosebud, and Cat stopped suddenly, it was because the river ended at a mountaintop lake covered in a faint blue mist. Lucy peered forward, but she couldn't tell how far the lake stretched. It simply seemed to disappear into the horizon. Since night was falling, Lucy decided it was time to go ashore and find someplace to make camp.

So she hopped out of the boat and splashed through the shallows, holding the boat's dock line (which is really just a fancy name for a plain old piece of rope) and looking for something to tie it to. She was happy to find a little dock that led to a nice straight road. It seemed too good to be true, but Lucy couldn't see the harm in making use of what she found. So, now soaking from the knees down, she clambered back into the boat. Lucy paddled a bit further, until the boat knocked perfectly up against the dock. She tied her boat securely to a piling (which is really just a fancy name for a thick piece of wood connected to a dock). Then she carried Cat up a tiny ladder, settled him on the sun-warmed planks of the dock, and returned to the boat for Rosebud, meaning to pull her gently through the shallows onto the little road (because cows do not do well with ladders).

But the cow would not leave the boat! When Lucy tugged at Rosebud's lead, the boat rocked, and Rosebud's narrow ankles quivered precariously. Rosebud did not like this one bit. She let out an obstinate bellow and did something cows never do. She sat down, awkwardly, so that her legs splayed out beneath her in a funny way. If Lucy hadn't been so tired she might have laughed. But she was tired, *so* tired.

"Suit yourself," she said to Rosebud. "You can stay here all night for all I care, and meanwhile Cat and I will go find someplace nice to camp. Someplace with delicious clover. We'll be sure to tell you all about it later."

And while it is true that such threats will not work on most cows, it is also true that Rosebud was a particularly smart cow. She stood back up, and when she did, Lucy frantically jumped up and down in the boat bottom, until it rocked in a frightening way (for a cow, anyway—*you* might have thought it was fun). Rosebud, with a short and surprised cry, tipped over and landed in the water. Lucy jumped in beside her, helped her up, and led her to shore, so that finally she was standing beside Lucy on terra firma (which is really just a fancy name for plain old dirt). Cat scrambled down the dock to meet them, and they all turned to face up the little road, which led directly into the densest, blackest forest that Lucy had ever seen.

It was a blot of ink, a puddle of spilled molasses, a solid swarm of wasps. The forest was so dark that it was impossible to make out individual trees, and Lucy had no way of knowing who or what lived within. She felt nervous when she saw it, without knowing why.

Hovering above the dark blur of trees was a heavy storm cloud. Lucy assumed it was the same storm cloud she'd noticed the day before from the bottom of the mountain. The last thing Lucy wanted was to head into a storm, but there was nowhere else to go. She took a deep breath and started along the path, toward the dense darkness and the heavy cloud.

When the darkness seemed to be directly above her, Lucy held up her hand to feel for raindrops. But the dusky night air felt clear and dry. She was puzzled but pleased, so she took eleven steps along the road, pulling Rosebud carefully behind her. Cat was unruffled by the cloud, but Rosebud seemed afraid. She peered anxiously up at the dark gray mass above her as she limped along on her sore hoof. The trees were very close—just a few feet away—when Rosebud stopped and bellowed. Lucy forced her on, pulling on the rope until the cow was almost choking.

"Come *on*, Rosebud. It's only a few trees. You can rest in a while, once we get somewhere with food, and maybe a soft place to lie down. See, Cat doesn't mind." Cat was ambling forward happily, sniffing every few feet. But Rosebud wouldn't budge. So Lucy let go of the rope and entered the forest with Cat at her feet, while Rosebud bleated sadly from a distance.

"See, girl. It's just fine. Nothing to be afraid of." But then, suddenly Lucy screamed—horrendously, loudly, painfully. *"Aggggghhhhhhhhhh!"* she yelled. Beside her, Cat let out a series of high, piercing barks.

Because the very second that Lucy and Cat entered the deep dark of the trees, cold rain and hail beat down on them. It felt like knives and nails were falling from the sky. The friends were pelted with chunks of ice, and needles of water poured from the strange cloud over the trees. The two ran quickly backward, and immediately the rain stopped. They fled back to Rosebud and stared in shock at the forest. Because it was *only storming directly over the trees.*

Lucy was stunned, and Cat had turned into a ball of wet fur at Lucy's feet. They all stood frozen, scared to move, and Lucy knew that they couldn't make their way into the forest until the storm ended. But now they were drenched, and the breeze by the lake felt terribly cold. Sleeping by the water didn't sound much better than running through the storm.

Lucy felt shaky on the inside, but she knew she had to take care of Cat and Rosebud. She stroked Rosebud's neck and then leaned down to pet Cat. But try as she might, she could not get the little prairie dog to uncurl. Cat just curled tighter and whimpered faintly in a way that made Lucy very afraid. "Please, Cat?" Lucy begged, trying to warm the little wet ball of fur with her damp skirts. "Please? Oh, Cat, what have I done?"

As if in response to her question, Rosebud nosed the pathetic ball of fur and looked at Lucy with a furrowed brow. Even Rosebud could see that Cat was very definitely not okay. Lucy and Rosebud sat for a minute, staring at the creature shaking on the grass. Then even the shaking stopped.

"Oh!" Lucy cried, afraid to say aloud what she was thinking. If Cat was beyond even his pathetic shaking, perhaps he was beyond any help Lucy could offer. But when Lucy buried her face in his damp fur, she could just make out the faint trembling that meant there was still life, still time. "Oh, Cat . . ."

Just then an even colder gust of wind came rushing off the lake, and Lucy knew they needed to find shelter. She guessed that the well-paved road through the stormy forest led to a town of some kind (or why would anyone have bothered to pave it?), but she knew that Cat couldn't go back into that icy storm, not even for a minute. Finally, she pulled Rosebud over to the edge of the road, to a small mound of grass. She carried Cat to the same spot and placed him carefully beneath the cow. Rosebud leaned down to lick Cat dry.

Lucy kissed both animals, looked into Rosebud's eyes, and said, "Stay here. I'm going to find help. Okay, girl?" Rosebud didn't respond. Lucy gently scratched the short fur between the cow's big brown eyes. "You're in charge, so take good care of Cat."

Then Lucy took a deep breath and steeled herself for the worst of the storm. She walked to the edge of the forest, so that her nose was almost inside the downward rush of water and ice. She counted to three and, without looking back, ran into the dark shade. She squeezed her eyes tightly shut, held her bag above her head, and galloped blindly down the road. She ran so fast that she could barely feel the pounding of the rain over the pounding of her heart. She squeezed her eyes so tightly shut that she felt like she was in a closet, but the closet was beating heavily all around her. The rain came from all sides, so that she could barely tell which end was up and which was the ground. She had no idea where she was heading, her only marker the feeling of the paved path beneath her feet.

All of a sudden, she stumbled. A bolt of pain exploded in her head as a tree stopped her mad dash. She hugged the tree, heaving for breath. As the pain in her head subsided, she realized that she couldn't feel the knives of rain anymore. She squinched one eye open and saw that she seemed to be momentarily out of the storm. She opened both eyes, rubbed her scratched forehead, and realized how lucky she was. The tangled branches of the tree above her were so thick that the rain couldn't reach her at all. The tree was so wide that there was room for her beneath its branches. She had found a nook in the forest, warm and dry. The tree had almost cracked her head in two, but now she was safe.

She peered out from her little dry safe place. Lucy had hoped that the forest was only a thin ring of trees surrounding a town or a village. But peering through the dark storm, she could not see the end of the trees, though she could almost see the lake if she stared back in the direction from which she'd come. In her little dry hollow beneath the tree, she felt safe, but there was no telling if she could find the sheltered place again or if Cat and Rosebud could make it through the storm this far. *If only they were here now,* she thought with a sigh. But she knew that wishing wouldn't make it so. *Or if only this tree were bigger. If only its branches reached all the way to the lake.* She sighed again.

Lucy dug around in her wet bag, although she knew exactly what it held. She fingered the thick wool blanket and thought that maybe she could stretch it over Cat and Rosebud. But she knew that it just wasn't enough to keep Cat and Rosebud safe. She took out the cup, but she couldn't think of any use for it. Then she found the knitting needles and all the brightly colored yarn. Some of the yarn had begun to unravel, and she pulled the loose purple tangle from her bag and onto the ground. She pulled and pulled at the loose end until there was a fluffy heap of yarn at her feet. *Useless!* she thought. *What was I thinking bringing my knitting along? As though I'd have time to sit and knit on this trip! Oh, if only I'd brought Papa's slicker instead.* While she wracked her brain, trying to think of a plan, she began to cram the yarn back into the bag. But a piece of it got caught on a stray stick that happened to be sitting beside her foot. She tried to untangle the stick from the yarn, but it was stuck fast. She stared at the mess for a minute, thinking a crazy thought. An odd idea was forming in her tired mind. She reached for her knitting needles.

She picked up a broken branch from the ground and wove it into the next line of stitches. The little scarflike thing looked strange with the stray stick hanging from it, but Lucy knitted faster. When she tugged at the stick and found it would not budge, she shrieked excitedly. She stood up on her tiptoes and reached for the lowest branch on the tree above her. Her fingers grazed a leaf. She pulled on the leaf until she could grab a twig and followed the twig with her fingers until she could grip the branch itself. She knitted it right into her yarn! When she ran out of branch, she cautiously stepped back toward Rosebud and reached for the next branch, which she knitted into the purple yarn as well. The two held and made a kind of tent. It seemed to be working! Lucy kept on like that, knitting, and whispering, "This will never work—this will never work—this will never work," knitting for all she was worth.

But eventually, the yarn ran out—because no matter how big the fluffy mound of purple had seemed, there wasn't enough to make it through the forest. And when it ran out, Lucy was still not even halfway back to Cat and Rosebud. She felt despair grow like a little stream inside her.

Lucy's arms and legs felt heavy. She'd never felt so tired, so sad, so lost. Of course, Lucy had felt bad before: confused about her mother, angry at her father. She'd fought with Wynston on a daily basis, and Sally too. Nothing was perfect, but this was new. This sense that she might be hurting two defenseless creatures—that her own impatience and stubbornness had led to this moment—was new. "There must be a way," she said sadly, looking at the limp, useless end of the last ball of yarn. But no matter what, she could not think of a solution. Meanwhile, she knew Cat and Rosebud were freezing in the open wind by the lake. She feared that without her, Cat might . . . fade further, might even . . .

No! She wouldn't think like that. There must be a way. She wandered a few feet back to see if she'd perhaps dropped a ball of yarn as she walked along. But no luck. No yarn. She doubled back again to the edge of her knitted

. . . knitting for all she was worth.

roof, and a stray hailstone bounced her way. She ducked to avoid it and tripped over a loose vine on the forest floor, skinning her knee. *"Aaaaaagh!"* she yelled. Couldn't anything go right? Dumb, dumb stupid vine! She tore it from the ground. And then . . .

Then she looked at the loop of vine in her hand. It was slim, strong, and supple, almost like a piece of rope. She tugged at it and saw that it led up through the trees. It was incredibly long, and when she pulled on it, the vine snaked down toward her, but she still couldn't see its end. *Hmmmm.*

Without an end, the vine was no use to her, so finally she just chewed into the strong green rope of plant. For a brief second she worried it might be poisonous, but there was no other option, so she pushed the thought into the darkest recesses of her mind. What was the worst that could happen? It couldn't be any more horrible than Cat's cold little body. Once she'd chewed herself an end, she tied the vine to the last little end of the purple yarn and began to knit. It was harder than working with wool, but not impossible. Yarn to vine. Vine to branch. Branch to vine. Her fingers flew. Her tiredness disappeared and her arms came alive again. She could save Cat!

After a few hours, and with a terrible cramp in her

fingers, Lucy collapsed on her back to rest. Her feet were stretched beneath the tent of her knitted canopy, but her head now lay outside the edge of the forest. She could see the stars. She couldn't believe it, but there it was—a safe path into the warmth of the trees. Not perfect, nor airtight. There were still drizzles of rain that made their way through her makeshift roof, but it was a lot better than nothing. She picked herself up, massaged her hands, briefly inspected her scraped knee, and slid the knitting needles back into her bag. Then slowly, tiredly, she walked out to Cat and Rosebud.

Cat was shivering, but his head was now visible. He stared at Lucy with frightened eyes and sucked on one of his paws. Lucy carried the prairie dog with both arms into the knitted forest, and Rosebud followed cautiously behind. Deep inside the tent of branches, they all curled up against the dry roots of the enormous old tree, and Lucy spread her blanket over them all. But after the adventures of the afternoon, nobody could sleep. Rosebud kept nudging Lucy's shoulder, and Cat tried to dig a hole in Lucy's lap. So finally, Lucy sang:

> *The soggy silly heavy rain*
> *is something to be seen,*

97

But I prefer a sunny day
  beside a speckled stream.
I like to keep the water
  where the water ought to be—
In a lake or in a pitcher,
  and the dryness all on me.

When Lucy finished singing, she looked around and saw that Cat was curled up in the crook of her arm, and Rosebud was sound asleep. Lucy shut her eyes and tried to think of happy things. *At the very least,* she thought, *the rain will have to be finished by morning. At the very least.*

About the time that Lucy was frantically knitting the last bit of yarn to the branches of a giant tree, Wynston was starting to get hungry. It was his third day (two and a half, if you want to be strict about it) of boring riding and he hadn't had a bit of hot food (or conversation) since leaving Willie the day before. He could see the lights of Torrent above him, but he decided to make camp anyway. "It's not polite to show up at a stranger's house for dinner," he told Sprout, "not even when you're carrying a letter from the stranger's son." Sprout just snorted and stamped, and Wynston took the snorting to mean *Let's eat,* and the stamping to mean *Hurry up, already!*

"I am hurrying," he said. "Hold your horses, Sprout!" Wynston laughed at his own joke, but Sprout was not amused.

"You've got no sense of humor at all," Wynston said indignantly while Sprout nosed at a rotting log. "Some company you are!"

Wynston built a small fire by the side of the road, and he munched on a few hard-boiled eggs and a slab of yellow cheese. He fed a carrot to Sprout, who then wandered off to find water. Then Wynston sat and stared at the fire and thought about things. After all, he had a lot to think about. Nothing in all his princely lessons, in all the books of etiquette, had prepared him for this adventure. Here on the mountain, none of the rules applied. He wondered how Lucy was faring without a horse to speed her journey. He stared around at the woods and noticed for the first time how silver the leaves looked in the firelight. He smelled the good dark smell of his campfire, felt the soft ground beneath him, and searched the night sky above the forest for his favorite stars. It felt good to be away, far from Thistle. Without his crown— in a dirty shirt and scuffed boots—he wasn't really a prince. Willie wouldn't have even known if he hadn't told him. Here, he was just Wynston, and that felt really nice. But he missed Lucy. He thought he could feel her nearby, but that was silly. Still . . . he hoped she was okay.

Missing Lucy felt almost like a bad stomachache, but the ache was in his chest and throat too. He felt lonelier than he'd ever felt before. Sprout whinnied gently, but it was little consolation. Wynston knew that if Lucy was hurt, or lost, it would be the worst thing in the world. He ate an olive, but the olive almost got stuck in his throat. He tried to make up a song, like Lucy, but he was terrible at it. He didn't get very far.

> Rain is wet, when it comes pouring
> Down on me, and that's just boring. . . .

Wynston had to admit he was no good at cheering himself up, at least not with songs. He considered the princess Halcyon, but that made him feel bad. He thought about the cold stone castle filled with golden things, and that didn't make him feel better either.

But when he thought of Lucy picking blackberries alone on a sunny Sunday afternoon, he lay down on the ground, smiled, and closed his eyes.

A VERY CIVILIZED PLACE

WHEN LUCY woke up to see the woven roof of branches, she only wanted to go back to sleep. Beyond the knitted ceiling, she could hear that it was still raining, though not half so hard as the night before. Rosebud was already awake, nibbling fallen leaves. Cat was sitting up a few yards away, staring hard at Lucy and making an impatient clicking noise. So Lucy dragged herself up, combed her damp hair with her fingers, folded her blanket, and realized she was starving! She snuggled Cat down safely into the driest corner of her less-than-dry bag, covered him with the driest side of the not-quite-dry blanket, tapped Rosebud firmly on the rump, and said, "Okay, Rosebud, it's time. Let's go. Run, girl!"

Lucy and Rosebud ran pell-mell down through the

soft rain. The path wound around the biggest trees, but mostly it ran straight and true through the forest. Since the sun was rising sharply, stretching its fingers through the forest in bright patches all over the mountaintop, tiny rainbows appeared everywhere, glinting and shifting, then disappearing as the light changed. Lucy could barely keep running, it was so beautiful. She wanted to stop and stare, but her hunger (which got bigger every minute) kept her moving. She and Rosebud ran and ran. Then very suddenly they bolted out of the forest and into a strange village, where Rosebud made a surprised *"Moo!"*

Lucy was startled too, but she kept running, making a left turn where the path forked into a spiderweb of circular sidewalks. She ran along the weaving walks until they led her to a gazebo at the place where the footpaths met. Only once she was under cover and could set Cat down did she stop to really look around her. When she did, what she saw took her breath away.

She was standing in the very center of a big round field, in a kind of bandstand or meeting place. The field all around her was covered with winding footpaths, each with its own little trellised roof. Grapevines and honeysuckle grew over each roof, so that the entire place felt like a maze, but also like a bouquet of wildflowers.

. . . they led her to a gazebo . . .

Each little path was exactly like the next, the same size and shape, and they were arranged in concentric circles. Lucy thought that perhaps, to a bird in the sky, they'd look like a rose, with the paths like petals carved into the mountaintop. She smiled at the thought.

Around the field full of footpaths was the village itself, a ring of adorable matched buildings. Each house was built of the same deep red stone, and the door to each house was painted the brightest shade of blue Lucy had ever seen. Beyond the village, a ring of tall, tall trees stood watch. So the gazebo was at the center of the footpaths, and the footpaths were at the center of the village, and the village was at the center of the stormy forest where Lucy had spent the night. Although it was sunny now, off in the distance hung a deep gray sky full of dark clouds.

From where she stood at the very center of the village, Lucy could see healthy roots growing through to the ceiling above her. She guessed that the roof of her gazebo was covered with honeysuckle, like the roofs of the paths. Everywhere, the town seemed alive, green and growing, and for a while Lucy was so entranced that she forgot about her growling stomach. She noticed that there were small green moths living in the roots dangling above her. She watched a few of them flit around her, and she felt calm for the first time since she'd climbed out of the boat. But soon the moment passed, and she felt *hungry* again! She couldn't help making up a little song, right there, on the spot.

I wish I could conjure up breakfast this minute. . . .
Maybe pancakes with jam, or an egg
    with cheese in it!
Maybe berries with cream, or a scone, piping hot!
Though I'll settle for oatmeal if that's
    what you've got. . . .

Lucy was just about to sing about fried potatoes with onion when she felt a tap on her shoulder. Startled, she turned quickly to find herself staring into the gray eyes of a young man about her age. He tugged on one of her damp curls. "Who are you, and what's that you're singing? If you don't mind telling me, of course."

Lucy gasped. "I'm Lucy." She jerked her head so that her hair flew out of the boy's hand. "And it's nothing—just a little song I made up."

"Why?"

"I don't know," Lucy answered slowly. "Just because I like to sing."

"Why?"

"Well, I've never thought about it before. Maybe because my mother liked to sing. Maybe I inherited it from her." Lucy paused to think about this, and it made her happy. "Or maybe just because I feel less lonely when I sing. Don't you?"

"I don't sing. I don't know how."

"Oh," said Lucy, though she couldn't understand how anyone could not know how to sing. She couldn't imagine it. "Well," she said, "okay then."

"Okay then," the boy repeated.

"Um . . . okay," Lucy said again. She stared at the boy, unsure of how to proceed. It felt rude to walk away, but Lucy was getting hungrier by the second. There was a long, awkward pause, which was broken by a rumble from Lucy's belly. "Uh . . . so, who are you?" she asked, hoping to distract him from the embarrassing sound.

"My name's Steven," said Steven. "Are you a stranger?"

"I suppose I am to you," replied Lucy, "though you're a stranger to me, too."

"But I belong here," said the boy. "And you don't."

"I've never been here before, if that's what you mean. But I'm not sure that not having been someplace is quite the same as not belonging."

"It is," said the boy simply.

Lucy wasn't sure how to respond. "Oh." Her belly rumbled again, and she rubbed it.

"So then you *are* a stranger!"

"I suppose I am."

His face lit up. "That's wonderful! I've never seen a real live stranger before." He peered very closely, and pulled a small leaf from Lucy's hair.

Lucy, a little uncomfortable, backed away from the boy. "I don't see how that's possible," she said.

"What do you mean?" asked the boy.

"Well, everyone's a stranger the first time you meet them."

"Yes, that's true," said the boy.

"And you have to meet everyone for the first time at least once. It only makes sense."

The boy looked stumped by Lucy's logic. He scratched his head. "I suppose so," said the boy. "Except that it doesn't."

"How's that?" asked Lucy.

"Because I know that my mother told me never to talk to strangers, and that was when I was very little. And from that day to this day, I must never have met a stranger, because this is the first time it's ever come up."

Lucy was a little tired of the conversation, and now

she was positively starving. "If that's true, you shouldn't be talking to me."

The boy thought for a second. "Yes. But you're my first stranger, and it's just too exciting. Besides, I'm a terrible child. Everyone says so."

"What do you do that's so bad?"

"All kinds of things. I'm a general nuisance. I break all kinds of rules."

At this Lucy chirked up considerably. "Me too! What do you do?"

"Well, sometimes I wear my socks on the wrong feet or I put my belt on upside down. Once I ate a buttercup, just to see what it would taste like."

Lucy thought of her own terrible mischief, and of how Thistle was likely to be reacting to her disappearance. She didn't think that the things Steven had mentioned made him a terrible child, but she kept quiet while he kept on talking.

"You know, you don't look like a stranger."

"How's that?" said Lucy, trying to be polite.

"Well, just different, I guess," said Steven. "I thought you'd look more different, but you just look like anyone, like my cousin. Only your hair is that strange color—"

"Oh," said Lucy. "I'm sorry, I guess."

"Don't apologize. You're pretty."

"Thank you, I suppose."

"But what are you doing here? People don't pass through Torrent very often, because it isn't on the way to anywhere. It's at the very top."

"This place is called Torrent? I've never heard of it."

"Then how'd you end up here?"

"Gosh—I was angry, I guess," said Lucy, "and I wanted to be somewhere besides where I was, and I wanted to see if I could climb the mountain . . . alone."

"Well, now you did!" answered Steven. "Is it all you thought it would be?"

"Hmm . . . I suppose. But . . . I also thought that maybe I could find . . . someone."

"Well, I'm someone," said Steven, which was true.

"I mean a particular someone," answered Lucy. "A person I knew long ago. She might have run away, or gotten lost, or something."

"Might have?"

"Well, I don't know. I don't really remember her— my mother."

"Your *mother*? Your mother ran away?" The way the boy said it, it didn't sound very likely. Lucy couldn't, staring into his strange gray eyes, think of any other mothers who'd run away.

"Well, I'm *almost* certain she did. It's a long story, but I think she might be up here somewhere."

"I like stories."

"Though my sister thinks that my mother is . . ."

"Is? What?"

"Is just . . . gone."

"Gone?" echoed Steven, confused.

"But I'm sure she isn't . . . gone . . . because I think that if she were, I'd know. So I want to see if I can find her."

Lucy desperately wanted to change the subject. "Even if I can't find her, I thought I might have an adventure, here on the mountain."

"What's an adventure?" asked the boy.

"What's an adventure?" Lucy didn't know how to explain. "An adventure is . . . a kind of journey."

"What's a journey?"

Lucy was a little shocked at the boy's lack of vocabulary. "It's a kind of a trip."

"What's a trip?"

Lucy really didn't know how to answer, and she was starting to feel a little cranky. She put her hands on her hips. "It's a lot like breakfast."

"Oh!" Steven didn't get the joke, but he understood breakfast. "Why haven't you eaten breakfast? Breakfast happens at seven-fifteen, and it's almost eight-thirty now."

"Is it? We skipped breakfast this morning. As well as lunch and dinner yesterday."

Steven looked shocked. "I didn't know you could do that, miss so many meals. Why did you?"

Lucy snapped a little. "We ran out of food. That happens sometimes, on an adventure. But I guess you wouldn't understand."

Steven looked hurt. "Oh."

"I'm sorry. I don't mean to get snippy. It's just that I'm starving. I've been in the woods for days and days, and I'm so hungry I could eat a cow!" Too late, Lucy realized what she was saying and bit her tongue. She looked guiltily at Rosebud, but Rosebud didn't appear to be listening. So Lucy continued, "But first I should really give Rosebud a good milking."

"Hey, I bet my mother would swap you breakfast for a pail of milk! I think that's an acceptable exchange," Steven said agreeably. "C'mon!" He began to walk through the rain to the door of one of the pretty red houses.

Lucy couldn't help thinking, as she followed Steven hungrily, that in Thistle, anyone would happily feed a traveler without considering acceptable exchanges. But she wasn't in a position to be picky, and she was happy to share a bucket of milk. She walked with Rosebud's lead in one hand and her bag held tightly in the other. Cat seemed to be sleeping peacefully in the bag, so she didn't bother to wake him up.

Lucy left Rosebud on the porch and followed Steven into a warm kitchen. A woman with Steven's same gray eyes was taking a loaf of fresh bread from the oven. Steven hung his hat on a hook by the door and called out, "Hey, Mom, look what I found in the Village Round—a real live stranger!" When his mother turned and saw Lucy, she jumped, but then her face softened.

"Oh! Who is she exactly?" she asked Steven, snuggling him warmly in her plump arms.

Before he could answer, Lucy, with a lump in her throat, replied, "I'm exactly Lucy." The cozy room reminded her too much of home. It smelled like soup. Something about the room and the bustling mother pushed all the words out of her in a rush. "I'm a milkmaid from Thistle, and I meant to find . . . someone . . . and have an adventure. But I'm very hungry now, and I think maybe Cat is sick, and I miss Wynston something awful, and nothing's gone quite right."

Lucy felt her eyes clouding over, and she hated the feeling. She hated it!

"Oh, ducky," said Steven's mom. "You look about to cry."

"I'm *not!*" answered Lucy. "I'm *fine!*"

"Lucy hasn't had a bite to eat for years and years," explained Steven. "She might even starve!" He looked excited by the prospect of such an occurrence. "She can pay us in milk."

"Oh, my duckling," said Steven's mother. "I doubt it's as dreadful as all that, but do have some bread and butter. I'll put on a pot of tea and we'll get you all washed up. Then you can do your milking. How's that?"

So Lucy washed her face, ate a good breakfast, and drank the warm tea until she felt much better. As she ate, Steven's mother bustled about her in a motherish way. This made Lucy feel a little sad, so she tried to think of other things. She said with her mouth full, "I've never seen a river that goes up a hill before."

"Is that how you got to Torrent then—on the river?"

"Yes, but it was an accident. Almost. What's it called, that river?"

"Why, that's the Current Current," answered Steven's mother matter-of-factly. "I've never been on it myself, never having reason to go anywhere but to the market."

"But how does one go down the mountain if the

113

river goes up so quickly? It would be awfully hard to paddle against it."

"Duckling, you should never paddle against the river, or against any river! The Current Current goes up the mountain on one side, and down the mountain on the other."

"I suppose that makes sense," said Lucy, remembering the map in King Desmond's throne room. It wouldn't really make sense if it went up both sides of the mountain, since the water would have no place to go.

"Things generally do, my duckling. They generally do." Steven's mother turned to bustle around busily at the sink, and Lucy finished her breakfast. As she was gulping her last gulp of tea, Steven's mother turned back around abruptly.

"I'm wondering, dear, who exactly you're looking for? We don't get many strangers in Torrent. There's really nobody out *there* who knows anyone *here*—which makes visitors rare."

Lucy set her cup down and took a deep breath. She was beginning to realize that this was a hard conversation, but she was also sure there was a clue waiting for her somewhere on the mountain.

"It's hard to explain. My mother was a goat girl long

114

ago. But she ran away, left the mountain, and moved to Thistle, which is where I'm from."

"Your mother? What was her name?"

"Nora. She was called Nora." Lucy's face was bright and curious. She held her breath. She held it and held it and held it, but . . .

"Well then, ducky, I'm afraid you've been misinformed. There's never been a Nora in Torrent as long as I've been here."

Lucy's face fell, but her hope held. "Maybe she just came from another town?"

"I'm afraid there is no other town on the mountain, dear. . . ."

"Not any?"

"Nary a one. There's only one town on this mountain, and the other mountains are uninhabitable, being made mostly of gravel and stone. In fact, that's why these hills and peaks were named the Scratchy Mountains in the first place—because it's mighty hard to scratch a garden patch from a bed of gravel and stone. All covered in pine needles and wind. Yes, it's mighty hard to make a life in these mountains, unless you happen to be a goat. So we're all there is, we Torrentians. Something of an oasis, our little village.

"But I'm afraid I'm confused as to the details. Why are

you looking for your mother here, if she moved to Thistle?"

"She isn't there anymore. She . . . ran away."

"Your mother ran away?"

"I don't know, not for sure. Nobody talks about her, ever. But I think she was homesick, probably, or maybe she'd done something—something wrong."

"And what makes you think that? I can't imagine any mother needing to be anywhere but with her baby chickens, and I can't imagine doing anything more wrong than running away from home." At this Lucy swallowed hard and looked at her feet.

Lucy thought for a minute, but try as she might, she couldn't think of anything but the goatherd song. She felt flustered. "I don't know. But she used to sing me a song at night before she ran away. And it was a song she'd learned on this mountain. I'm sure of it. So I wanted to see the mountain, okay? There's something here, some part of her. I feel it."

Steven's mother just turned back around and began to sweep the hearth as Lucy hummed the song. She didn't seem to be taking Lucy very seriously at all, but she listened. "That is indeed a Torrential tune, but maybe she just learned it from someone else."

"But . . . ," Lucy floundered.

"Why don't you go and tend to your milking, my duckling."

But now that the conversation was out in the open, Lucy couldn't stop herself. "Maybe she just lived here before you came to Torrent?"

Steven's mother paused with her broom in the air. "No, I've lived here all my life, and I assume I'm about as old as your mother would be. So no . . . there's never been a Nora."

"Oh." Lucy didn't know what else to say. So she took a bucket out to the porch, where she found Rosebud munching happily on the fresh grass growing between the floorboards of the porch. She milked Rosebud, and as she milked, she thought about how things can change quickly. She felt her mood shift.

The storm had been horrible, but Torrent was not a bad place, despite the drizzle. She liked Steven and his mother, and she thought the flowers that seemed to be growing everywhere were beautiful. Just as she was feeling better, a terrible scream rose from the little red house, and Lucy ran inside quickly.

"Get it out, out! Catch it *now!*" Steven's mother was shrieking and running around the room, knocking things over, and wringing her hands.

But just as Lucy stepped into the room, Steven

turned a bucket over onto the tile floor of the kitchen. His mother crumpled onto a chair and covered her eyes with both hands. "Take it out now. I might faint. Oh dear, oh dear, oh dear. Nothing like this should ever happen. And in my tidy kitchen too! Take it to the jail, Steven. They'll handle the horrid thing." Steven slid a thin wooden cutting board beneath the bucket and carried his makeshift trap through the back door of the kitchen to dispose of whatever was causing the ruckus.

"What was that thing?" asked Lucy. "Are you okay?"

"Barely! Oh, my duckling! Just be glad you were outside. It was terrible," she whimpered. "It was so terrible, so terrible and so *wild*."

"What was it?" asked Lucy. "A mouse?"

"No, no! Not a mouse, though that would be dreadful too. This was far worse. Oh, I hate to even think of it. It was a big thing, with long awful teeth and the most snarly face!"

"It sounds just awful," said Lucy. "We had a rat once in the barn at the dairy, and I hated its beady eyes. Sally wouldn't even look at it."

"Oh, this wasn't a rat. It was much, much bigger," said Steven's mother. "I've never seen anything like it. It was like a wild dog, with great razor teeth and terrible claws. I stepped on it, and it growled at me—the most awful, bloodcurdling sound. Who knows what it would have done if Steven hadn't been so quick?"

But Lucy felt her heart sink. Suddenly she was certain she could imagine just what the beast looked like. She was sure she knew the sound of its bark. She held her breath and reached into her bag for Cat, but she was not surprised to find the bag empty. Her heart sank.

"Ma'am—maybe it was a nice beast?"

"Oh, duckling, you're so young. There's no such thing as a nice beast."

"B-but, what do you think they'll do with the animal? The terrible beast?" Lucy tried to keep calm. She wanted to run after Steven, but she had a sense that claiming the animal as her pet would not win her any points with Steven's mother, who seemed convinced that Cat was a terrible monster.

"Why, they'll hold it until nightfall and then set it loose . . . ," began Steven's mother. Lucy felt slightly better, until Steven's mother continued, " . . . in the Pit. They'll leave him to the hailstorm just like they do with any other criminal, according to the sound laws of Torrent. Thank goodness!"

"The Pit?"

"Yes. It's an old system, to be sure, but it never fails. Some things can't be improved upon, you know?"

"What kind of a pit?"

"Oh, it's just your average pit—a big well of sorts, but without any water. Dug deep down into the floor of the forest. It goes down about forty feet on the sides, and the bottom always has a few inches of mud in it. It doesn't drain properly, not at all."

"But why? I mean, why did somebody dig a pit into the mountain?"

"Oh, there's all manner of myths about it. Some say it was once a fire pit for a giant monster, a great scaly beast called the Bludgeone. But, of course, that's silly. Most believe it was a cistern, a great vat for water storage. Only, it drains down through the mountain, so it was no good for storing anything. Except beasts. For as long as I can remember, and for a long time before that, it's been used for exposing wild beasts and other terrible types. Criminals."

"It's full of bones!" added Steven, hopping cheerfully back into the house and the conversation. "It's like a big cup, with a puddle at the bottom. A puddle full of bones!" He grinned.

"Ah, Steven, back so soon?" asked his mother. "That's my speedy boy!"

Lucy gulped. "But what if you're wrong? What if the animal isn't terrible? What if it was a sweet animal—maybe even someone's pet, like a cat."

At this Steven's mother shook her head. "Perhaps you're addled, love. I know what I saw, and it was not a cat."

"But you know what I mean." Lucy was very frustrated. "An animal you like, that lives with you. A friend."

"But it wasn't," insisted Steven's mother. "It was wild. A beast!"

"But someone might love it. It might be a nice beast. . . ."

Steven's mother lost her temper. "*No!* It might not. And I don't want to talk about this any further! There wouldn't be a law against wild animals if wild animals weren't a bad thing. And the hail wouldn't come at night if bad creatures didn't need to be punished. That's how things work in a very civilized place. Just be thankful for the order of things."

Lucy felt she had pushed too far, and was fast wearing out her welcome. When Steven's mother turned her back to scrub the spot on the floor where Cat had stood briefly, Lucy left. She untied Rosebud from the porch and walked off in the rain to find the jail. Just when her skirts had almost dried, things seemed to be getting soggy again.

WILD RAVENING BEASTS

ABOUT THE time that Lucy was standing in the gazebo with Steven, Wynston was waking up from his third night of camping on the mountain. And if his first night spent sleeping beneath Sprout was a little awkward, and his second night was generally uncomfortable, his third was downright painful. He had been tired enough to fall asleep on the gravel-strewn ground, but not tired enough to stay asleep peacefully. Now his back felt like he'd fallen down the castle stairs at least eight or nine times, and he couldn't stop yawning. Needless to say, he had had enough adventuring.

The rain was misting as Wynston rode quickly through the forest into town. He hoped to deliver his letter, find Lucy, and head home by lunch. He was beginning to feel a prickly kind of nervousness at being gone so long. He'd had too much time by himself, time to imagine the things his father would do to him when he returned. While he was ready to face the tempest, he felt strongly that he needed to do it now, before he lost his nerve. So he hurried through the town. He didn't know where to find Mrs. Wimple, but the town was fairly small. He thought he'd just try each house until he found the right one, or a friendly person to direct him.

But the first house he approached had a sign on the door that said THE ASTER FAMILY, so he didn't knock on that door. Then the house next door read MR. AND MRS. FARNSWORTH BARNACLE, so Wynston moved along to the third house, on which there was a particularly impressive golden plaque that read HOME OF COSIMO C. CALLOW, MAYOR. It was hard for Wynston to believe that the town was actually alphabetized, but when the sign on the fourth house read DR. DELIA DISTRESS, Wynston got back on Sprout and rode through the light misting rain until he thought he might be nearing the Ws. He located the Wimple residence, tied Sprout to the mailbox, and knocked on the door.

Persimmon Wimple's house looked much like the rest of the houses in Torrent, red stone with a lush garden growing on the roof, but Wynston barely noticed. He was feeling moist, and he thought that perhaps Mrs. Wimple would offer him a dry place to sit, and maybe even something hot to drink. But just as he was imagining a mug of cider and a freshly ironed shirt, the door swung open. A large woman with a tear-streaked red face cried out, "Oh, what now? For goodness' sake, what now-ow-ow-ow?" Then she fell into Wynston's arms and sobbed. Mrs. Wimple, who looked rather like her son but with gray braids that fell to her knees, stopped crying just long enough to sputter, "Th-th-thank you, my boy, for the c-c-c-comfort, but wh-wh-who are you anyway?"

"I'm Wynston, a friend of Willie's. I've come to bring you a letter," replied Wynston. "But I can come back later, if now's a bad time."

"Willie? You have a letter from Willie?" snuffled Mrs. Wimple. "Why, that's the best news I've had in weeks." She stopped crying and wiped her nose with one hand while she pulled Wynston into the small house with the other. She shut the door and fell heavily onto a couch by the fire, where she dried her face on a pillow.

"A little rainy today, isn't it?" Wynston said, attempting to make polite conversation.

Mrs. Wimple stared at him for a minute, and then she replied, "Only as rainy as usual."

Wynston didn't understand. "Oh. Does it rain much in these parts?"

"It rains the correct amount each day," said Mrs. Wimple more cheerfully. " 'Storm by moon, dry by noon,' just like in any very civilized place."

"What do you mean by that?" asked Wynston. "It doesn't rain the same each day in Thistle. Some days it rains all day, and some days it doesn't rain at all."

Mrs. Wimple looked vaguely upset, and then amused. She chuckled to herself and twirled one of her braids in the air. "I'm sure it does, darling, I'm sure it does. And do the people of Thistle all know how to fly as well?"

Wynston didn't like to be treated like a little boy. After all, he was almost a man, and a prince to boot. "No," he answered. "Of course not, but I promise you—the weather isn't on a rigid schedule at home. Just ask Willie."

This confused Mrs. Wimple. "That doesn't sound orderly at all. What a mess it must be there. Are the people all in a muddle all the time?"

"No," said Wynston. "It's fine." Though as he said this, he considered that it would be rather convenient to know in advance when to expect a shower, or a snowstorm.

"But however do you get along if the weather changes from day to day? How do you know when to wear your galoshes?"

Wynston shrugged. "Sometimes our feet get wet, but then we dry them off."

Mrs. Wimple shook her head. "Next I suppose you'll be telling me that you don't bother with clocks either, or regular meals, or those pesky days of the week." Wynston thought this was silly, and he tried to tell Mrs. Wimple so, but she continued, "And that reminds me, it's the proper time for morning tea. Would you like something?"

Wynston nodded. Regulated rainstorms and alphabetized houses were a little odd, and crying mothers were very sad, but a snack was an altogether welcome thought.

After Mrs. Wimple had made tea and set out a plate of cookies, Wynston handed her the letter from Willie. She slid it carefully into her pocket and then sat down again with a sigh. "Ah, Willie! If only he were still around to help me, things would never have gotten so bad. I'm sorry you found me in such a state earlier, but I've been having a tough time since Willie's father passed away."

Wynston looked up from his tea and mumbled through a mouthful of sugar cookie, "Gosh, I'm so sorry to hear that, Mrs. Wimple. What happened?"

Mrs. Wimple tied her braids into a knot beneath her chin and closed her eyes. "It really isn't something to discuss with the young, but I must admit it's nice to have someone here to chat with." She took a deep breath. "The problem is that I'm out of money, and I owe seventeen thickles to the town market, which is quite a lot of silver. I've been taking in sewing, and I was beginning to catch up. But last week the mayor sent over the collector director, who told me I have to pay the seventeen thickles by today, or va-va-vacate the premises." Mrs. Wimple's chin began to quiver, and she looked like she might burst into tears again. "I'll have to move in with my sister, I suppose, but that will be so humiliating. Oh, how she'll gloat!"

"Why don't you just ask for a little longer to pay the thickles back, so you can do some more sewing?" This seemed common sense to Wynston, who reached for another cookie.

Mrs. Wimple blew her nose. "I don't know about in Thistle, but there's no bending the rules in Torrent," said Mrs. Wimple. "Laws are important. Don't you know that?"

"I certainly do!" Wynston nodded in a most royal manner. His years of training filled his head. "I can recite the bylaws of Thistle by heart."

"Well then."

"But even so, throwing you out of your house seems a little harsh."

"Harsh or not, a law is a law."

"I suppose so . . . ," said Wynston. But he wasn't entirely sure. It just didn't seem right to him.

Wynston thought of his kind, if blustery, father, the king. And though he knew his father prided himself on fair rule, he also knew there'd be a way to help Mrs. Wimple if she lived in Thistle. He couldn't imagine his father throwing a widow into the street. He thought to himself, *Surely there's a solution to such a simple problem . . .* but he didn't say anything. Instead he went outside to check on Sprout. He needed some time to think about things. His quick visit to Torrent was becoming more complicated by the moment.

But however complicated things were feeling to Wynston, they seemed far more complicated to Lucy. Glad to see that the rain seemed to be letting up, she moved as quickly as one could with a cow in tow. She didn't know exactly where she was headed, but Torrent was a small town, and extremely well organized. At every intersection were little signs pointing the way to the town's most important sites, so after she had passed the first few signs reading TOWN HALL/HABERDASHERY, and ICE CREAM PARLOR/THE JAIL, she knew exactly where she was going. Once she had found the jail, it took her no more than a minute to find the right window to peek through. But the minutes felt like years to Lucy, who was very worried. Finally, by standing carefully on Rosebud's back and craning her neck, she caught a glimpse of Cat, who was locked in a wire cage about the size of a bread box.

Cat had curled into a ball again, and two men stood over him. One of the men was tall and thin, and he wore a very shiny suit and a fancy red hat. The other man was unbelievably short and muscle-y, and he wore a uniform. The short man in the uniform kept poking Cat with a wooden spoon. Each time he jabbed the spoon, Cat curled into a smaller ball of fur and shivered a little more.

Then, just as she had while knitting the forest, Lucy forgot about her mother. She forgot about Wynston. She even forgot about herself, because she had a GIANT job to do. This was a serious grown-up decision she had to make on her own. How could she possibly help Cat? She felt scared but brave as resolve filled her. She clenched her fists, ready for a fight. She wasn't sure just what she had to do, but she knew she had to do something.

She climbed down and led Rosebud around to the front door of the jail, where she found two signs. The first read sternly THE LAW PROTECTS THOSE WHO PROTECT THE LAW. The second proclaimed FLAVOR OF THE DAY: BUTTER FUDGE RIPPLERUMP! Lucy puzzled at this. It didn't seem very Torrential to sell ice cream in a jail, but she was learning not to be surprised at the twists and turns of her strange adventure. She knocked on the door and then walked into the jail. Inside, it was cold and damp. A glass case with a giant bin of ice cream sat beside a small desk. On the desk were a feathery quill and a heavy chain.

"Hello?" Lucy called into the damp room. "Hello? I believe you've found something that belongs to me. Is anyone here?" Of course, she knew someone was inside the jail, but she didn't want the two men to know she'd been spying through the window.

The short man came out to meet her, carrying his spoon. He smiled in a friendly enough way, smacking the spoon lightly against the palm of his hand. "I am, of course. Who might you be?"

"I'm Lucy," said Lucy.

"Ah, so you are. What brings you to town?" asked the man. "Were you wanting a scoop? Because if that's the case, I'll have to disappoint you. I'm not permitted to serve this until after lunch. It wouldn't be good for your teeth or your appetite."

"Yes," said Lucy. "It does seem a little early for anything fudgy."

"Indeed. But if you don't want a frozen confection, why are you here?"

"I'm looking for someone," answered Lucy.

"Really? You have relations here?" The man looked surprised.

"Oh!" said Lucy, who had been thinking of Cat, and not her mother. But . . .

"Perhaps a cousin, or an uncle?" The man leaned in with his spoon to stir the ice cream.

"Yes, or . . . maybe . . . but . . ."

"And who might that be?"

"My mother, Nora. Her name is Nora. Do you know her?"

The man straightened up and licked his spoon. "No, there's no Nora in Torrent."

"Yes," answered Lucy, "that's what I heard." She felt sad, but not nearly as sad as when Steven's mother had said it. She had Cat to think about now. She might wish and hope and dream for her mother, but Cat needed Lucy, and that was even more important right this minute.

"Well then, why are you here, shouting like this? I thought you said you'd lost something. . . ."

"Yes, there's that too. In fact, *that's* why I'm here. Not Nora. Not right now."

"Well then. Say what you mean. Address the matter at hand, my girl! What sort of a something have you lost?"

Lucy put on her sweetest face and tried to sound like Sally. "A very special something. A terribly important something. I think perhaps you've found my Cat."

The short man nodded sympathetically. "Oh, goodness. That's very sad, very sad indeed—a lost kitty. But we haven't found a cat, I'm sorry to say—"

Lucy smiled her prettiest smile as she continued, "Are you sure about that? Steven's mother mistook him for a wild beast and trapped him, but he's my pet. I found him at the bottom of the mountain. He hates to be cold—hates it awfully—so if you'll just let me have him, I'll take him home to Thistle right away."

"Miss, surely you aren't referring to that animal Steven brought in! We don't know quite what that wild, ravening beast is, but he's no cat."

"But, sir," said Lucy, who had truly begun to think of Cat as a cat, or at least a pet of some kind, "why do *you* get to decide he isn't a cat? Maybe the cats in Thistle are different from the cats here in Torrent. Maybe he's just a different kind of cat. Maybe he's part cat, or maybe—"

The short man interrupted. "Maybe I'm a mermaid! Maybe it'll snow in June! Maybe may be a lot of things, missy. If you found him in the wild, that rightly defines and categorizes him under Torrential law as a wild beast. And under code seven of bylaw 784J, wild beasts are criminals. Such crimes are punishable by immediate midnight exposure on the south side of the forest."

The man with the spoon said all this in a surprisingly cheerful voice, which Lucy found confusing in light of the very serious situation at hand. She didn't know how to respond.

"But—" she said.

"Button your jacket!"

Lucy was confused. "So—" she whispered.

"Sew buttons!" the man chortled and smiled.

"Oh, sir, isn't there any way I can take him home?"

" 'Fraid not," said the man in the uniform pleasantly. "What you need is a nice goldfish in a bowl, or a pet geranium. My son has a very well-behaved geranium named Bernard."

The idea that a geranium could ever replace Cat made Lucy so angry that she stamped her foot and walked back through the door without even saying goodbye. Lucy made up a song as she walked, to calm herself. She sang quietly through her clenched teeth.

> Men in silly uniforms
>   who get to make the rules
> Should all be poked with wooden spoons
>   and sent away to schools,
> Where wild beasts will teach them
>   that it's better to be free
> Than it is be a grown-up,
>   stiff and stubborn as a tree!

"Ooh! I'll find a way to get Cat out of that nasty old jail," she told Rosebud quietly as they passed through the center of town. "I will, I will, I will. If only Wynston were here, then everything would be different. They'd listen to a prince, I bet. Not that I need him, but it would be nice. . . ."

At the exact moment she was thinking about Wynston, Wynston was thinking about her, and a kind of magic happened. The magic of coincidence. The magic of perfect timing. Just as Lucy was stomping furiously across the town square and Wynston was stroking Sprout's nose on Persimmon Wimple's front porch, the rain stopped. When the rain stopped, the sun came out. And when the sun came out, all the doors of Torrent opened like clockwork.

Like clockwork, each child in Torrent ran out to play in the dry noon-hour sun. Like clockwork, each grown-up stepped out into the yard. At every house, a woman poured a pitcher of milk into tall glasses and a man planted a tray of sandwiches in the exact center of a picnic table. Lucy stopped where she was standing and stared. She thought it was the strangest thing she'd ever seen, stranger than the orange flowers or the river that flowed up the mountain.

Wynston stopped and stared too. He glanced around at the houses, but then he saw something even better than the mechanical lunch scene, and he smiled. His face lit up and he jumped into the air with a yelp and yelled, "Lucy! Hey! Hey, Lucy, I'm here! I came to find you! Hey, Lucy! LU-CY—"

Rosebud heard Wynston's voice and snorted happily. Lucy heard Wynston, turned, and ran toward him with open arms. The villagers of Torrent heard Wynston's loud, happy voice and had no idea who he might be, but were rather concerned with the disturbance to their lunchtime schedule. Lucy and Wynston didn't care one bit. They hugged each other tightly, and then they began to argue.

He shook his finger in Lucy's face.

Wynston looked at Lucy with a half sneer. "What were you thinking, running off like that? I would have come too, you know." He shook his finger in Lucy's face.

Lucy remembered very suddenly that she was supposed to be angry at Wynston. "Maybe I didn't want you along after you forgot me on Sunday, you noodle-head. Where were you, anyway?" Lucy demanded. "Off studying how to part your hair on Tuesdays? Or maybe you were practicing your proper pucker, at a lesson in princess-kissing?" She puckered her lips in a horrendous kissy-face.

"It wasn't my fault—" began Wynston, blushing at the talk of kissing. But when he tried to offer her his explanation—about the sticky lock on the ruby-room door, and how he'd actually spent his entire Sunday trapped in the rare-jewels tower—Lucy shushed him.

"Oh, Wynston, forget it. I don't have time to stand here arguing with you."

"What?" This took Wynston by surprise. Lucy always had time to bicker.

"It doesn't matter right now. Truly. I think I need your help with something."

Wynston had never before seen Lucy's forehead wrinkle in such a worried grown-up way. He wrinkled his own forehead before he said, "What is it? Are you hurt?"

"No, not me," Lucy grouched. "I'm just fine. I can take care of myself, you know. I got all the way up the mountain alone."

Wynston ignored this. "Then what could possibly be so bad? I mean, this place is kind of neat, isn't it?"

"Neat? It's creepy, if you ask me."

"But it's so organized. . . ."

"*Ugh!*" yelled Lucy. "You *would* think that—you with your shiny shoes and your silly laws. Not everything fits the rules, Wynston. This place is *bad.*"

Then the entire story poured out. Lucy told Wynston about finding Cat, and about knitting the forest during the terrible storm in the trees. She told him about the boat, the river up the mountain, and the boy with the gray eyes. Finally, she told him about code seven of bylaw 784J. When she was done, she sat down on the moist grass beside Rosebud. She looked intently at Wynston.

"How's that for laws?" she asked.

"Pretty bad," admitted Wynston. "Pretty awful."

"And don't you see, this is all my fault?"

"Oh, Lucy, that's not true. . . ."

"I should have stayed home. If I hadn't run off, Cat would have gone back to wherever he came from, and Rosebud would be grazing with the herd in the field behind the dairy. Sally is going to be furious with me, and who knows what my father will say. I've made a mess of absolutely everything. Your father was right!"

"No!" said Wynston, in a loud, firm voice.

"And probably I won't even find my mother."

"Your mother?" asked Wynston. "What about your mother?"

Lucy blushed and waved her hand, as if to shoo away the conversation like a fly. "Oh, never mind that."

"No, Luce. What about your mom?"

"Oh, it sounds silly out loud. But that's why I came . . . looking for her."

"But, Lucy, isn't she d—"

Lucy cut him off before he could finish his sentence. "Do you know that, Wynston, really know it? Have you ever actually heard anyone say it?" She stared him down carefully.

Wynston had to admit he hadn't. "No, but . . ."

"Well then . . ."

"But, Lucy . . ."

"No! No buts, and no more wasting time chattering. Cat needs us now. I never should have come here. Mother or not. Even if I find her, it isn't worth this . . . awfulness."

Wynston sat down on the grass beside Lucy. He

thought for a minute before he spoke. "But, Lucy, your crazy adventure has made all kinds of other amazing things happen. If you hadn't run off, I wouldn't have pulled Willie from the stew pot, and he might still be stuck there, too hungry even to wiggle his legs. And I wouldn't have come to see Mrs. Wimple, so there'd be nobody to help her find the seventeen thickles she needs. Good things are happening too."

Lucy shook her head, confused. "Who's Willie? What's a thickle?" Wynston began to explain, but Lucy interrupted. "Oh, Wynston, I don't know what you're talking about, but can it wait for later? If I can't rescue Cat, they'll put him out in those woods. And what they do—it's the worst thing, and so cold. I don't even want to tell you. Oh, Wynston, if that happens, he'll die. I swear he will! If you had seen him during the storm, so afraid, and curled into a little wet ball—"

The look on Lucy's face was the saddest thing Wynston had ever seen. So he quickly stood up and held out his hand to Lucy. "Well, c'mon then. I'll tell you about my adventures later. Right now, we'll go see what the Prince of Thistle can do about the bylaws of Torrent. There's got to be a way to fix this mess."

"Oh, I hate to have you get involved."

"That's silly, Luce. We're friends, and friends help each other."

"But this is my awful mess, so I should be the one to fix it. I can't have you just traipsing in there with your crown and . . . hey! Where *is* your crown?"

Wynston rubbed his floppy hair sheepishly. "I . . . um . . . I lost it."

"You what? Oh, your dad is going to go nuts!" Lucy was gleeful for a second, but then she got back to matters at hand. "Anyway, like I was saying . . . this is my mess, not yours."

"That's silly," replied Wynston quickly. "Just think of all the times you've saved me, thinking up clever ways to get me out of trouble with my father or helping me study for my stupid lessons. You do all kinds of things to help me. Can't it be my turn this time?" Wynston pleaded.

"Oh, rats!" Lucy knew she was beat. "Just so you know, I hate this. But do you really think you can?"

"Laws are complicated, but this will work out. It has to."

Lucy wasn't so sure, but she smiled and took Wynston's hand. He pulled her onto her feet and she grabbed him around the neck, hugging him so hard he squirmed. "I'm sorry I ran off, Wynston. And I'm pretty glad you showed up, you goofy toad," she whispered in his ear.

NO ROOM FOR WIGGLING

LUCY WALKED back to the jail, holding tightly to Wynston's hand. This time, she didn't bother to knock, but pushed the door open so that it clattered against the wall. She stomped into the room, dragging Wynston behind her. She felt stronger, more able to shout. She was glad to have Wynston along. "Hello?" she called out impatiently. "Helloooooooo?"

The short man scurried out from the back room again, this time without his wooden spoon. "Yes, yes, what can I help you with—" he started to say. But when he saw Lucy, his tone changed. "Oh, it's you again." He made a very grown-up face, as though he smelled something funny. "And I see you've brought a friend along this time. How nice for me."

."In fact, it *is* nice." Lucy drew herself up as tall as she could. "I have brought a friend with me. And I think that maybe you'll change your tone once you've met him. He's *somebody*."

Wynston wasn't quite sure how to react to the uncomfortable introduction, but he remembered one of his father's General Rules of Kingship: *No honest man can resist a real smile and a true handshake.* So he stuck out his hand. "How do you do? My name's Wynston. Nice town you've got here, sir."

The short man hesitated, but then he smiled and reached forward to shake Wynston's hand. "Hello yourself. And don't bother with the 'sir.' Everyone just calls me Chief, though really my name's Bertram. We wrote an amendment to make it my official title. So I've got two legal names." He beamed proudly. "How do you like that? I'm chief o' police, and we run a pretty tight ship here in Torrent. I'm sure the little lady's already informed you."

Wynston was surprised at the friendly reception. After Lucy's tearful description of the jail, he was expecting something far meaner. The chief didn't seem like an especially unreasonable fellow, just a man doing his job. "It seems that way," he said cheerfully. "Nice to meet you, Chief!"

"Likewise, I'm sure." Then the chief stood silent for a minute or two, rocking back and forth on the balls of his feet. Lucy waited for Wynston to fly into action, and Wynston waited for something to happen.

Finally, Lucy got tired of waiting. "Um, about my Cat . . ."

But this was exactly what the chief had been waiting for, and he launched into the same speech Lucy had heard earlier.

When he was done, Wynston spoke slowly. "Hmm. Sir, I'm what you might call a prince."

"Well, isn't that nice for you. I don't think I've ever met a genuine prince before, though I've read about them in very old books."

"My father is king of Thistle, and so that makes me a prince."

"True enough. That's the way it generally works." The chief waited.

"So I thought perhaps . . . uh . . ." Wynston faltered.

"Yes?" The chief's face grew stern.

"I thought you might . . . um . . . make an exception for my friend here—and her Cat." He finished his sentence quickly, spitting it out.

"An exception?" The chief looked as though he'd

never heard the word before. "An exception, you say?"

"Yes, well, that's what I was thinking, if it isn't any real trouble."

The chief's face hardened. "I'm afraid it is a real trouble. I'm afraid it might cause all kinds of trouble. Exceptions generally do. That's precisely why there are *no exceptions* in Torrent. None. Not ever."

Wynston wasn't sure what to say next. "I see," he finally answered.

"I'm glad. That makes things easy." The chief stood still for what seemed like a very long time.

"But then, do you think I might talk with your king for a minute?" begged Wynston. "I won't take much of his time, I promise."

The chief folded his arms in front of him as he spoke. "There are no kings in Torrent."

"No kings?"

"Nope. No exceptions and no kings. No wild beasts and no lawbreakers. And there is *no room for wiggling* when it comes to these important matters! You can't run a civilized place if lawbreakers and wild beasts and exceptions and silly kings are running all over making a mess."

"But—" Wynston was baffled.

"But what?"

145

"But what's wrong with kings?"

The chief sighed. "Let me see if I can explain. Torrent is a civilized place, guided by the will of the people. Kings are cruel men who abuse powers they haven't earned." He raised his eyebrows slightly as he leaned over Wynston. "Do you understand me, *Prince*?"

Wynston was flustered. "Um—who's in charge here—I mean, who makes the laws, if there isn't a king?"

The chief answered as if reading from a very dull book. "The good people of Torrent govern the good people of Torrent, in abidance of laws set forth by the good people of Torrent."

Wynston thought, *Clear as mud.* But aloud he said, "How does that work, exactly?"

"It's very complicated, and would take me all year to explain our constitution. Checks and balances. Vetoes and votes. Very complex, but basically, we govern ourselves. We keep each other in line."

"You mean there isn't anyone in charge here? That sounds like it must be very confusing, with everyone running around deciding everything at the same time."

"Not really," answered the chief, "and besides, the people of Torrent don't run around. They walk slowly, except in cases of great emergency."

"I'm sure." Wynston nodded his head. "But what about you? You seem awfully important. You aren't even a little bit in charge?"

At this, the chief's expression shifted momentarily. He fingered a medal on the front of his uniform and said softly, "Well, there are some folks who would say the town couldn't run without the chief. Some folks *do* say that."

"I'm sure they do," said Wynston. "How'd you get to be chief?"

The chief puffed his chest out and slapped it with his spoon. "I was appointed."

This didn't make sense to Wynston. "But if nobody is in charge, then who appointed you?"

"Our fine mayor!" said the chief proudly.

"A mayor?" asked Wynston. "What's that?"

"The mayor is in charge of settling the rare grievances that occur, interpreting laws, and signing decrees. Incidentally, he also plays the tubatina in the Torrent Symphony Orchestra."

"But doesn't that make him a little like a king? Not the tubatina, but the other stuff, the laws and decrees. Isn't he doing the same thing a king does?"

"Not at all," the chief replied, shaking his head. "It's an elected position. More fair, and far more civilized."

147

"Oh, I'm sure," said Wynston, who was not sure at all, but didn't know what else to say.

"I'm glad you understand."

"So everyone gets a turn to be mayor?"

"Well, not everyone. But anyone *could* be mayor, if they wanted to be—if they were at least thirty-seven years old and born in Torrent, as well as nominated and elected by a two-thirds majority."

"I see, and how often does the mayor stop being the mayor?" asked Wynston. "I mean, how long has this particular mayor been the mayor?"

"Hmmm. I can't say precisely. Mayor Callow's been around for a long time, maybe about twenty years now. Time flies, you know. And it's hard to remember exactly—since our last mayor was also called Mayor Callow."

"The same name?" Wynston looked puzzled. "That's an odd coincidence."

"Not so odd, since Mayor Callow was the father of Mayor Callow, before the people of Torrent elected Mayor Callow to be the new mayor."

Wynston thought this sounded familiar, a lot like how a prince became a king. He smiled. "It all makes a lot of sense. But what if somebody not related to Mayor Callow wanted to be mayor?"

"Oh, I suppose they could make some signs and have a party, but I don't see why anyone would ever oppose a Callow. The Callows have experience in these matters."

"He does sound great," said Wynston. "I'd love to meet him. Do you think we might get a chance?"

"Well, I don't see why not," said the chief. "The mayor's a most friendly fellow. Wait here, and I'll go fetch him." And so saying, he turned and wandered into the back room, whistling as he went.

While he was gone, Lucy bit her fingernails, and Wynston pondered if perhaps there weren't some laws in Torrent that really didn't make sense. Then he thought of his father, and of the Queening process. Just as he was beginning to untangle a knot of tricky thinking, the chief returned with a tall man in a fancy hat.

"Well, well!" said the man in the fancy hat as he strode into the room importantly. He leaned over Wynston and held out his right hand as he twisted his impressive mustache with the fingers of his left. "What have we here? Distinguished visitors from the lowlands, from other parts of the Bewilderness? I'm impeccably pleased to make your acquaintance!"

"And we're very glad to meet you too," said Wynston. "I'm Wynston, the crown prince of Thistle, and this is my very good friend Lucy. She's a milkmaid, and a talented one at that."

"I'm sure she is. I'm sure she is," replied the mayor. "Nothing like a cold glass of milk, that's what I always say. Now, what can I do for you good people?"

Wynston eyed the chief, who stood in the doorway that led to the back room. He was beginning to think that maybe Lucy was right about Torrent's system of justice, but he held out hope that the mayor, like his father, was a good man and a fair leader.

"Well, sir," said Wynston, clearing his throat and speaking in his best regal manner. "It seems that you've confiscated Lucy's cat, and we're hoping you might return him to our care. We promise to leave town immediately, and not to cause you any further problems."

"Lucy's cat, is it?" The mayor peered over his very long nose at Wynston. "A cat you say? A cat?"

"Yes, well, perhaps he isn't quite a cat, but his name is Cat. Anyway he's a pet all the same."

"A pet?" The mayor looked at the ceiling, adjusted his hat thoughtfully, and repeated himself. "A pet?"

"He's a pet, according to Lucy!" Wynston insisted.

The mayor smiled a funny little smile. "Hmm. I suppose that the animal in question is a pet—only if the word *pet,* as established by the laws of the land, indicates the animal in question. Wouldn't you say?"

"I suppose," supposed Wynston.

"Let's go over the facts, shall we?" Wynston and Lucy nodded hesitantly. "When in doubt, pay attention to the facts, that's what I always say! Don't you agree? Firstly of all, the creature was found in the wild, which makes him a wild beast. Isn't that so?"

"Only—" Lucy opened her mouth to argue, but the mayor continued.

"Secondly of all, he doesn't look like a cat, which is what you'd have us call him. Isn't that also true? Thirdly of all, he makes a very disagreeable noise, an obvious indication of uncivilized ways. Yes, all the evidence points to the fact that Cat is not a cat at all, but rather a ferocious animal. And one must pay attention to the facts, that's what I always say!"

"We know. You already said that," Wynston broke in. "You already told us that's what you always say."

"Did I?" asked the mayor. "Well, it's true, you know. The facts don't lie!"

Wynston looked back at Lucy, who was chewing on one of her curls and wrinkling her forehead. He wanted to help, but had no idea what to do. Nothing in his princely training had prepared him for a negotiation like this. But he hated to let Lucy down, so he tried again. "Sir—Mayor Callow—don't you think that this one time you could make an exception?"

"Exception?" snorted the mayor. He reacted much as the chief had reacted only a few minutes before. "Have you even seen this beast? Do you know what you're asking me to do, young man? Bertram, bring that thing in here!" The mayor snapped his fingers, causing the chief to scurry into the back room. He returned immediately, carrying a grimy old metal cage. In the cage was a trembling ball of fur.

"Cat!" Lucy cried. At the sound of Lucy's voice, the ball of fur uncurled, and Cat's head appeared. He tried to stand, but the cage allowed him only to sit up slightly. He stuck his nose through the bars of the cage and sniffed sadly. Then he clutched the bars with his little paws and attempted to chew through the lock.

"Do you see what I'm dealing with?" The mayor gestured toward the cage and faced Wynston. "Look at those teeth! You can't possibly expect me to turn this animal over to a sweet young lady like Miss Lucy here. Who knows what might happen?"

Lucy was feeling anything but sweet. She'd been

keeping quiet while Wynston tried his calmer method, but finally her temper burst. She sputtered out, "You are a horrid, horrid man, Mayor Callow! You must have no heart at all! What kind of town puts an innocent animal to death but allows mean old men in silly hats to prance around telling everyone what to do?"

At this, the mayor turned a cold eye on Lucy. "We have an old folksong here in Torrent, a song we like to sing about beasts like yours." He sang:

> *Wolves will howl, and bees will buzz,*
> *But wild is as wild does.*
> *So keep your village free of beasts*
> *Except when roasted for a feast.*

He sang in an odd nasal voice, and it was not a pretty sound. It was not what Lucy thought of when she thought of music, but the mayor seemed pleased with himself.

Wynston tried one last time. "Mayor Callow, you seem like a reasonable man. Won't you please let Cat come home with us? Please?"

"No, I'm sorry." The mayor clapped his hands together in a most official manner and gestured to the chief, who removed the cage, hoisting it awkwardly as he scuffled to the back room. "It's simply out of the question. Laws protect those who protect the law. That's what I always say!"

"That's what you always say! That's what you always say? 'That's what I always say' is all—you—ever—say! You know, you can't *always* be saying *everything*."

The mayor's face turned red. For a minute he looked as though he might yell, but then he went back to twirling his amazing mustache calmly. His voice took on a frighteningly even tone that made Wynston look at his feet, though Lucy met the mayor's icy gaze dead-on, with a fiery stare of her own. The mayor spoke in an almost scary whisper. "Temper, temper, that's what I always say. If this is how you're going to behave, young lady, I believe we're more than done here. Unless you have any other laws you'd like me to break for you? Hmmmm?"

But now Wynston remembered the sad tears of Persimmon Wimple, and he tried to speak again, for Willie's sake. "In fact, sir, there is one more thing."

"Is there? You don't say! You want something? I'm absolutely shocked and astounded. You don't *seem* the type to make ridiculous demands." The mayor snorted through his mustache. He seemed bored with the conversation. "And just what might this one more thing be?"

"It's about Persimmon Wimple."

"What about Mrs. Wimple?"

"I believe she owes you some thickles. I'd like to help her, but I don't have any money."

"Well then, you'll be of little help." The mayor turned to leave.

"I was wondering if you might accept my horse in place of the money." Wynston spoke in a rush as Lucy whipped her head around to stare at him. He glanced at her puzzled face, but kept talking. "I'm a friend of her son, Willie, and I told him I'd look in on her. I'd never forgive myself if she was turned out of her home."

"Actually, my boy, that is within the parameters of the law. A horse is an acceptable exchange for the taxes on Mrs. Wimple's house, assuming that the horse is healthy and well behaved."

"Oh, he's the best horse you'll ever meet!" Wynston cried.

"Assuming that the horse is a horse, and not some rhinoceros that this young lady found in the woods." The mayor stared hard at Lucy, who stared back twice as hard and chewed on her bottom lip some more. "You see, I'm not cruel or evil. I'm not an unreasonable man—and the laws of Torrent *do* work, and we *are* fair. You see?"

Wynston couldn't believe he was losing Sprout so quickly. "Um—his name's Sprout," Wynston said. "Right now he's tied to Mrs. Wimple's front porch."

"Fine. Fine," said the mayor. "I'll take care of everything."

"You will?"

"Yes, and may I say that it's a delight to see you following the expected protocol. Perhaps you aren't completely uncivilized, down there in Thistle."

Wynston bristled a little at this, but the anger wasn't nearly enough to overcome his sadness at the loss of Sprout, or his relief at being able to help Mrs. Wimple. "Please be gentle with him," Wynston begged, "and remember that he enjoys a carrot every now and then. Also, don't forget to scratch his nose. He likes that too!"

But the mayor was finished listening. "You're both dismissed. I've wasted enough time, and now I have real work to do. Good day." He turned his back and left the room.

Wynston could barely look at Lucy, who could barely look at Wynston. They walked from the jail quietly, shutting the door behind them.

THE END OF THE ROPE

LUCY WALKED over to Rosebud. She put her face very close to the cow's ear and said something Wynston couldn't hear. Rosebud licked gently at Lucy's hair. Wynston left them alone. Then Lucy untied the cow's rope, and she began walking calmly away from the terrible jail.

Wynston followed closely behind, watching Lucy curiously. They walked that way for a while, down the street to the edge of the forest. Then Lucy stopped, spun around in a circle, and waved her arms until she felt better, which took about six minutes and thirty-seven seconds. Then Lucy stood still until her dizziness passed. Finally she turned to Wynston, who was staring in amazement at the whirligig before him.

"Gosh. I'm sorry about Sprout," she said. "That's

awfully good of you. Who's Mrs. Wimple? Who's Willie?"

"It's a long story," said Wynston, trying not to think about Sprout. "They're just some people I met. I'll tell you all about them some other time, but I don't really want to talk about it right now."

There was an unusual silence then, a quiet space between them that lasted a long moment.

Wynston fidgeted, and the silence broke. "But hey, I'm really sorry about Cat. He looks really nice. I don't think he seems a bit mean or bitey, though I also don't think he looks much like a cat."

"Yeah, I know. But thanks."

"And you can't say you didn't try, right?"

"I guess, but . . ."

"So," said Wynston, "where's this boat of yours?"

"What?" Lucy looked up, surprised.

"The sooner we get to the boat, the sooner we can get away from this nasty place."

"But, Wynston, we can't just leave!"

"I know it's sad, but I don't guess we can do much else."

Lucy snapped. "That's one way to look at it, I suppose—the weakish way!"

"What do you mean?"

"I mean," said Lucy, "that this place has stupid laws. I don't intend to let Cat die in the forest just because of that horrible man."

"Lucy, you can't possibly hope to . . ."

Lucy didn't wait for him to finish. "I can't? I can't, can't I? I've learned a lot here on the mountain, no thanks to you. And maybe I didn't find my mother, and maybe I won't . . . but I'll kiss a blue baboon before I'll desert Cat."

"Lucy . . ."

"Because I know what it's like . . ." Lucy choked a little. "I know what it's like . . . to be left behind."

And Wynston could not say anything to that.

Finally Wynston shook his head. "You are absolutely, positively, without a doubt the most impossible milkmaid in the entire world! You can't just show up in a strange town, break all the laws of the land, and then run away."

"Watch me, Wynston."

"I know it's awful, Lucy, but there are reasons for those laws. What if everyone broke them whenever they wanted?"

Lucy snorted. "Go back home, Wynston, to your princesses and your daddy and your tiny forks. Go home." She turned to walk away.

"Lucy!" Wynston called after her. He was so confused. He knew he was right, that laws were there for a reason. But he knew that what Lucy was feeling was also right. Maybe there were different kinds of right. Maybe right in Torrent was different from right in Thistle. And Lucy's right was always a little different from everyone else's right. It all seemed terribly complicated, but he knew—more than anything else—that he couldn't let Lucy down.

"Hey, Lucy, okay! Okay!" Lucy looked back at him. "But even if we want to save him, how can we possibly sneak Cat out of that jail without the mayor and the chief noticing?"

"I'm not sure."

"So is it really worth it to get caught if the chance of success is that slim?"

Lucy opened her mouth to yell, but then she shut it again. She took a minute to gather her thoughts. When she finally spoke, she spoke carefully. "Wynston, I know it sounds silly and impossible and ridiculous and all, but I came here to look for my mother, and instead I found Cat. When we were hungry at the base of the mountain, I promised Cat and Rosebud I'd get them home, and I want to keep my promise."

"Lucy, I'm still not quite sure where you got this idea

160

to look for your mother—or what makes you think she isn't dead—but if saving Cat is that important . . ."

That word. That big word, DEAD, sounded to Lucy like a clock stopping, like a heavy rock hitting the ground. Wynston didn't say gone, he said DEAD. And he said it before Lucy could cut him off, or wiggle out of the conversation. Her face turned to stone when she heard it. Nobody, nobody, had ever said that word before, not about her mother.

"Lucy?" Wynston looked softly at Lucy, but Lucy had had enough.

"I'm fine!" she exclaimed. "But I have work to do here. And you . . . you . . . just you never mind my mother. This isn't about her."

"It isn't?"

"It's about you. You stood me up. I came here to get away from *you*, remember?"

Wynston looked hurt, but he couldn't fight back. He knew Lucy was muddled up inside, and that what she was saying wasn't altogether untrue. Even though it wasn't altogether true either.

"Lucy?" He reached out a hand to her. But she flinched away.

He tried again. "Lucy?"

Then Lucy came to her senses. She reached back, touched his arm, and said in a most un-Lucy-like voice, "No. That's not true. Not really . . . but look, I can't think about all of this now. Not with Cat in danger. I'm sorry that I got you into this, and if you'd like to head back now, I'll understand. But I can't go home. Not without giving it a good hard try."

"Okay, then."

"And I might have to break the law. Because I'm not a princess, remember? It doesn't so much matter what I do, because I'm not suitable anyway."

Wynston frowned. "What? What do you mean, not suitable?"

"I'm not suitable. Your father said so. . . . I'm not . . . not a princess." She stared at him as she said it. "But I understand, and it's okay. You can't help that, and you can't spend so much time with me anymore. Because you need to find someone suitable."

He reached over to pull on one of Lucy's curls. "Oh, applesauce! We'll just see about that."

"What does that mean?"

"Nothing important," said Wynston. "C'mon, let's go get your beastie."

"Really and truly?"

162

"Really and truly, you silly milkmaid. Let's do something unsuitable."

Lucy didn't know what to say. "Thank you, I think."

"Listen, Lucy. When Sally told me you'd run off, it gave me the worst feeling I've ever had."

"It did?"

"It really did. And if something bad happened to you because I left, I'd feel like a monster."

Then Wynston and Lucy looked at each other, and it was strange and quiet and new and uncomfortable. Lucy looked at Wynston, and she thought he seemed older and wiser. Wynston looked at Lucy, and he thought she was the bravest person he'd ever met. The gaze lasted a few seconds. Lucy almost hugged Wynston, and then she almost slapped him. Finally she decided against both, and she just laughed. So Wynston laughed too, and things felt normal again. "Besides, with Sprout gone, I'd have a long, boring walk home. So I guess I'm in for the jailbreak. But let's be careful, hey?"

Lucy stuck her tongue out, but Wynston could tell she didn't really mean it. "Suit yourself! I don't care what you do!" she called out as she ran back toward the jail. Wynston followed close behind, holding Rosebud's rope.

Back at the jail, they patted the heavy stone wall and

bickered in hushed tones about the best course of action. Wynston's first idea was to dig a tunnel under one wall of the jail and up through the dirt floor inside the back room, where Cat was trapped, but Lucy argued (quietly) that the tunneling would take too long, and by now it was really starting to rain again.

Lucy thought that maybe Wynston could distract the mayor and the chief while she darted stealthily inside, released Cat, and then quickly ran back out. But Wynston reminded Lucy that she wasn't as quiet or sneaky as stealthy burglars are generally rumored to be.

"Pooh to you," whispered Lucy, but she dropped the subject.

Then Wynston suggested that they ring the town fire alarm and create a huge ruckus to draw the mayor out of the jail. But it didn't seem likely that the wet town of Torrent had many fires, so it didn't seem likely that they'd have a fire alarm. Not to mention that the villagers of Torrent didn't exactly seem the ruckus-y type.

Finally Lucy sighed, which caused Rosebud to amble over in concern. Lucy leaned against the wall, stroking Rosebud's nose and fiddling with her lead rope. Meanwhile, Wynston clambered onto the cow's back and peeked into the back-room window, slipping slightly on her rain-soaked hide. "Hey, Lucy," he said. "Hey, Luce—climb up here. You aren't going to believe this."

"What is it now?" Lucy looked up, worried. "Are they poking him with a fork this time?"

"Not even close. No forks in sight, but Cat's loose back there. He's out of the cage, and nobody's in the room with him."

Lucy looked up at the window. "What did you just say?"

"It's true, he's bent the bars on the cage and gotten out. Only, they've closed the door to the front room, so he's stuck back there."

Lucy climbed up beside Wynston. The added weight made Rosebud grunt, but Lucy didn't notice. She stood gingerly on her toes, looked around the jail room, and saw that Cat was indeed loose, licking himself neatly beside the cage. Cat glanced up at Lucy and Wynston, then resumed his bath. "Some wild beast!" she exclaimed. "You can see why everyone's so terrified. Just look at that ferocious animal! He might eat the whole village in one mouthful."

As if in response, Cat chirped out a friendly *"Owrfuf!"*

Wynston said, "Shhhhhhhhh!" to Cat, and then he turned back to Lucy. "So now what?"

At first Lucy thought to climb in and back out again

with Cat. She even hoisted herself up into the window, but the drop to the room was nearly six feet. While she was willing to risk the fall, she didn't think it was likely she could make the climb back out. "Let me think," she said, pausing on the sill.

Wynston peered in too, studied the drop to the jail-room floor, and whistled. "That's a long way down," he said. "But it's an even harder jump up. I just don't see how it can be done." Wynston sat down on the cow with his face in his hands. Rosebud shifted awkwardly, and Wynston apologized.

Lucy thought hard, but there didn't seem to be many options. "I suppose," she said from her perch, "I suppose that if I can get in, I can pass Cat out to you. Then maybe I can pull that table over to the window and climb out myself." She looked into the cell and thought about whether the table would be too heavy. "I think I can do it."

Wynston fiddled with the fur on Rosebud's back. "And what do I do if you get stuck in there?"

"You run as fast as you can back home. You take Rosebud and Cat, and you follow the path to the boat. You'll have to manage to get around those rocks on the other side of the lake, but once you're on the downriver slope of the Current Current, you're home free."

"But if you came up one side of the mountain by the river, how do we know where we'll end up if we go down the other side?"

"Oh, no," said Lucy. "It's not like that. It's the strangest river. It runs up one side, and down the other, but then the two streams are connected in a kind of circle around the base of the mountain. Almost like a moat. We took a little bridge that crossed over it, when we were walking. Very *civilized*." Lucy made a face. "Haven't you ever looked at the map on the wall of the Great Hall?"

"Not really," Wynston had to admit. "But I believe you. . . . So, then what?"

"Then you run like the wind. It's not far from the base of the mountain back to Thistle, if you get off the river-ring at the right place. I think." Lucy gulped a little, hoping she was right. "And there's no other boat tied to the dock right now, so I don't think it will be possible for the mayor to chase you home."

"Don't be ridiculous. I can't leave you here!"

"I hope you won't have to, but at least that way Cat will be safe. And what if they do catch me? They won't dare put a girl out in the woods at night, and if they do, it won't kill me. And then I'll find my way home— somehow." Lucy decided it was better if Wynston didn't know about the finer details of Torrential punishment—the bones or the puddle.

Wynston tried to think of another solution, or at least a convincing objection to Lucy's plan. He hated to think of leaving Lucy if she got stuck in the jail, but there was no point in arguing with her once her mind was truly made up.

"I really hope you know what you're doing," he said, looking up at where she wobbled precariously.

"I hope so too," she replied. Then she peered in at Cat, who had finished his bath and was staring up at them. Cat's nose twitched, and he held out his paws toward the window. Lucy angled her legs in through the window. "I'm coming!" called Lucy. She briefly looked down at Wynston, waved goodbye, and then shut her eyes.

"Wait!" Wynston cried, but as he held up his hand to grab her skirt, Lucy wedged herself through the narrow space and was gone in a breath. Wynston stood back up on his tiptoes, balancing on Rosebud's sturdy back, and looked down at Lucy, who now resembled a pile of damp laundry on the floor.

"I'm okay!" she called out weakly. "I'm just fine." She pushed herself up into a sitting position and rubbed her knees.

... *Lucy wedged herself through the narrow space and was gone in a breath.*

Wynston watched as Cat ran over to Lucy. The furry beast crawled into her lap and made a funny clicking sound. Lucy snuggled her face down onto Cat's head for a minute and made kissy noises. Wynston, frightened, whispered, "Hurry up, Goosey!"

"All right already!" Lucy looked around. "Hey, Wynston, I have an idea. Throw me down my bag, just the bag!"

Wynston pulled out the knitting needles and blanket, which he tossed onto the wet grass beside Rosebud. Then he gently dropped the bag down through the small window. "Look out below!" Lucy looked up, caught the bag, and held it open next to her on the floor of the cell. Cat crawled obediently inside.

"Now the rope!" she called out softly.

Wynston looked around for a length of rope, but the only one he saw was tied firmly around Rosebud's neck. "You mean Rosebud's rope?"

"No, the rope that's tied to the bucket at the well in Thistle." Lucy sighed. "Of course I mean Rosebud's rope."

Sheepishly, Wynston tossed the end of Rosebud's lead into the jail. It dangled a few inches over Lucy's head. "No need to get snarky at a time like this," he said.

Lucy ignored Wynston, reached up on her tippy

toes, and tied the rope around the handle of the big shoulder bag. She watched closely as Wynston hauled Cat through the window. He leaned down, hung the bag over Rosebud's neck, and waited to see what Lucy would do next. Cat poked his head out and nuzzled Rosebud.

Lucy looked around her. The room held only the metal cage, the heavy wooden table, a set of manacles bolted to the stone wall, and what looked to be raisins but were likelier petrified rat droppings. She shuddered at the thought of spending a night in the bare room and took a moment to cross her fingers. Then, quickly, she carried the cage over to the spot beneath the window.

But when she tried to stand on the cage, it buckled beneath her weight. "No wonder Cat managed to get loose. I guess they don't often have wild beasts in Torrent. This cage probably hasn't been used in centuries."

"C'mon, Luce!" Wynston called softly from above. "Take forever, why don't you."

"Oh, hush!" Lucy walked over to the table and pushed, but the table wouldn't budge. She tried again, but it didn't move an inch.

"Want me to come down? Maybe we could move it together and then both climb out."

"Nuh-uh. Stay where you are and keep an eye out for

the chief," said Lucy. "I think I can get it." She held her breath, closed her eyes, and heaved with all her might. She felt the table shake for a minute, and then it moved an inch. She pushed harder, and it moved about a foot. But as it did, it gave a horrible, terrible, awful screech. Lucy froze when she heard a noise far worse than the screech. From the next room, she heard a voice.

"Where there's noise, there's trouble, that's what I always say!" announced the voice.

Lucy ran back to the window. "Wynston!" she called. "Someone's coming. Run for it!"

"Wait," said Wynston. "Grab hold!" Then the rope fell back down and floated in the air above Lucy's face.

"Don't be stupid. You can't possibly pull me up."

"Just shut up and grab hold!" Wynston insisted.

Lucy heard footsteps in the doorway and did as she was told. She grabbed tight. "I'm ready!" she whispered loudly. Then she heard the terrible sound of a sweet young milk cow being poked with a knitting needle, and suddenly Lucy was jerked up and through the window. She flew, scraping her face and arms on the wall as she went, and then she banged both elbows on the windowsill as she hurtled out into the rain. One minute she was sailing through the air, and then, THUNK! She was on the damp, soft grass. "Run!" she yelled, and she ran. Wynston raced along close behind her, and Rosebud, still yelping in pain, kept a few steps ahead.

They made for the trees, leaving behind one knitting needle, a rather damp blanket, and a mightily confused mayor. As they neared the path through the forest, Lucy heard shouts coming from the jail. "In here!" she called as she made for the path beneath the knitted canopy of the forest.

With everyone running as fast as they could, there wasn't much time for paying attention. So when Lucy felt a pull at her neck and cried out, Wynston and Rosebud ran on ahead. They left her, without meaning to, tangled in a hawthorn vine, pricked and scared. She could hear the sound of someone behind her on the little path. She struggled against the branches, but the more she pulled, the worse the tangle got.

She wrestled with the vine at her neck, but only succeeded in getting the hawthorn snaggled in her hair. Voices were getting louder, and feet were thundering closer.

"Oh," she said. "Oh, snappit!" She wrenched her hair free, leaving a good bit behind. Wincing in pain, she stepped off the path and a few feet into the wood, trailing bits of vine and bramble with her. She ducked behind a big old oak tree when she saw the mayor, the chief, and a small herd of Torrentians coming down the path. But there was no time to waste, and so she moved, as quickly but quietly as she could, through the forest. She was just a few feet from the path and a few feet ahead of the crowd, within sight of the paving stones but under cover of vines and branches.

The path was longer than she remembered, and Lucy could hear the sound of heavy feet on it, but she crept along fast, picking her way through the trees, her clothes askew and her hair full of brambles and knots.

Behind her, though, something interesting was happening. The vine that had become tangled in Lucy's hair was connected firmly to one of the vines holding the knitted canopy together. And as Lucy made her way, she began to pull the stitches loose with her. The canopy was unraveling like a sweater. As it unraveled, the branches gave way and began to sway and snap back into their usual positions. Behind Lucy, tree limbs flew and tore into place, and the roof quickly disappeared. Nuts and twigs rained down onto the Torrentians, and they were very much afraid and confused. They watched as order became disarray and Lucy, only a few feet ahead and a

Nuts and twigs rained down onto the Torrentians . . .

few feet off the path, ran for all she was worth. The crowd moved more slowly than one little girl desperate to join her friends.

When Lucy burst out of the forest, Wynston was standing on the little dock, looking strangely puzzled. Lucy couldn't understand why he wasn't in the boat, why they all weren't in the boat—and then suddenly, horribly, the truth struck her!

Lucy realized something very bad, something even worse than very bad. She remembered that the boat had been just perfect for a Cat-size dog, a young cow, and a girl named Lucy. But it was far from perfect now. Lucy stared at the tiny vessel as she moved toward it. She stared at the rocks across the water. She stared back at the path, and then Lucy stared at Wynston, who noticed her and threw up his arms as if to say *Now what?*

There was no more time for delay. *"Get in!"* she yelled as Wynston clambered, holding the Cat bag, into the boat bottom.

"But—" said Wynston as he reached to untie the boat. "But, Lucy?"

"I know," she said as she made her way down the rickety planks of the dock. "I know, but I don't know what to do."

Just then the crowd, led by the chief, burst into view. Lucy was standing with Rosebud at the very edge of the dock, which was small and shaky. The boat had drifted a few feet away from her. The Torrentians were closing in, but more carefully this time. Several pieces of wood had already splintered off the dock, and the rest promised to do the same.

"Move with care, people," the mayor was saying. "Easy does it. That's what I always say."

Lucy grabbed Rosebud's neck and began to push her toward the water. There was now a good ten feet of open water between the dock and the boat. She couldn't think how to get the cow from the dock into the boat, especially now that it was drifting.

"Lucy, what are you doing?" called Wynston from the boat.

"I'm staying here, and you're taking Cat and Rosebud. Back to Thistle. As fast as you can!"

"No, Lucy!" shouted Wynston, with no time to spare. "No." There was steel in his voice, a tone Lucy had never heard before. "Do you know what they'll do if they catch you now? Now that you've broken the law? Jump in and swim to the boat!"

"But that isn't right!"

177

"No, it isn't. But I'm not even sure we can get Rosebud into the boat anyway."

"We have to at least try. This isn't fair!"

"Sometimes things aren't fair. Swim!"

"No!" cried Lucy.

"Yes!"

"But I got us into this mess."

"Yes, you did," said Wynston, "but now you need to get us out, *fast*!"

Lucy shook her head. "I can't."

"Yes, you can. And Rosebud will understand. There's no more time for fuss. Jump!"

Lucy looked at him, and then down at Rosebud, whose eyes looked bigger and sadder than they'd ever seemed before. She wrapped her arms around the young cow's neck and whispered into the warm flesh, "I'm so, so sorry, girl."

Rosebud made a low sound in her throat and turned her head to look at Lucy once more. It broke Lucy's heart.

"Wynston!" she called. "If I do this, you need to swear we'll come back. You need to promise we'll come back as fast as ever we can, and fetch her."

"Lucy . . ."

"*No!* You need to swear, or I'm not coming."

178

"Lucy, it's a long way up the mountain, and my father . . ."

"Forget your father and his rules for once. Forget you're a prince, and swear it! You're my best friend, and I love you." Lucy choked on this difficult word. "I love you, and if you love me, you'll swear." She stood and stared at Wynston, who stared back for what felt like forever. The crowd was finally reaching the dock, and there was no time left to haggle.

"I swear it!" he finally called. "I swear to you, Lucy. We'll come back right away."

At that, Lucy untangled her arms from Rosebud, gave the cow a quick kiss on the neck, and whispered a heartfelt promise in the young cow's soft ear. "I'll be back, girl. I will." Lucy dove into the water, which hit her like a bolt of cold lightning.

Although it takes a while to tell this story, all of it happened in the blink of an eye and then, just as suddenly, it was over. The boat was in the water, Wynston and Cat were safe, Lucy was swimming, and Rosebud was standing, lonely, on the shore.

You aren't really leaving me? her soft brown cow eyes seemed to say.

Lucy gripped the side of the boat and pulled herself

up. Once she was safe, she pummeled Wynston with her fists.

"Oh! What are we doing?" she cried.

Rosebud was a sweet beast, and smart for a cow. Still, she was a cow. She couldn't really begin to understand what was happening. She waited patiently for something else to happen. The boat drifted further out, and the cow craned her neck, reaching out in the only way she could. She had followed Lucy a long way, and now only wanted to follow her further. She took one step at the edge of the dock and tumbled forward, somersaulting awkwardly, to land knee-deep in the water. She *moo*ed sadly.

"Wynston, I changed my mind—we can't do this!" yelled Lucy when she heard the sad sound of Rosebud calling. She grabbed the second paddle and began to stroke with all her might, so that the boat turned in a pathetic circle. But the boat wouldn't go back to the shore. Lucy dropped the paddle, reached out her arms, and then waved, sick at heart, to Rosebud. She blew kisses as the boat began to move away.

"Oh, Wynston, this is bad. So bad," she said in a hollow voice.

"I know it is, but I promise we'll come back. We'll

come back soon, and then we'll get her home safe . . . somehow."

"I forgot how small the boat was."

Wynston looked at the scene on the shore, and tears filled his eyes. He stared at Rosebud, who was now at the mercy of the herd of Torrentians.

"She's a good little cow, Lucy, and it's awful, I know. But I think she'll be okay. Just look." Together they watched as the crowd teetered out to the water's edge, grabbed hold of Rosebud's rope, and began to pull on the cow. Lucy could hear the small throng of people arguing over what to do with the cow. Over the hubbub, they could hear the mayor's voice clearly. "Settle down, folks. Good riddance to bad rubbish, that's what I always say! Look at it this way—a free cow!"

"But . . . ," Lucy said.

"You can feel bad later if you want to, but right now you need to help me. Lucy, paddle. I mean it!"

Finally Lucy looked up, her eyes grim and her jaw set. She noticed that the boat was drifting sideways and that Wynston couldn't manage both paddles on his own. She picked up a paddle and dipped it into the water.

"Rosebud!" called Lucy. "I'm so, so sorry! I love you, sweet girl. I'll come back for you just as soon as I can."

181

Rosebud heard Lucy's voice carrying across the water, and she struggled to free herself. She arched her neck and shook her big soft head. She couldn't understand what had happened, but when she saw the little boat pulling far out toward the edge of the mist—when she saw that Lucy had turned her back and was paddling away—her gentle cow heart broke.

And all of the villagers stopped pulling and stared at her. Because when Rosebud cried, she made the saddest sound of all. And nobody could believe it.

"Loooooooooooocyyyy—!" called the cow. But Lucy was gone.

DOWN AND DOWN
AND FURTHER DOWN

THE SMALL crew just paddled sadly for a while, missing Rosebud and Sprout and feeling stunned. Once they were far enough away to be sure nobody was chasing them, Lucy dropped her paddle. She slumped, her fingers trailing in the water.

Wynston felt awful too, but he knew that Lucy felt worse, so he busied himself by moving Cat-in-the-bag to the far corner of the vessel. Then he stared at the huge jagged rocks all around the boat. Luckily, the boat was not rushing toward the perilous stones but floating lazily along. Wynston examined the situation. When the next rock was within two feet of the boat, he gently pushed it with his paddle, so that they drifted forward and away from the rock. Within seconds, another rock threatened and Wynston did the same. "This isn't so hard," he murmured to himself. "Not bad at all."

"That's because you're doing it all wrong!" Lucy's voice broke sharply through his concentration. She had unslumped herself. "Let me try!" Lucy wiped away her tears and pushed Wynston out of the way. "You have to hold it like this!"

Reluctantly, Wynston handed over the paddle. "Okay, but look out! There's one right there," he called, as a rock nearly crushed his side of the boat.

"Of course there is, and I almost missed it because you're distracting me!"

"Sorry," said Wynston. He wasn't really very sorry, but he knew Lucy was having a hard time. "Are you okay, Lucy? You don't need to pretend. If you feel sad, you can—"

"I can't concentrate with you yelling all the time!" snapped Lucy as she pushed the boat away from the next ragged patch of stones. "Hush up!" Wynston understood. Lucy wasn't mad. She was just trying not to cry.

For the next hour, the little crew navigated the obstacle course of stones, but they were pleasantly surprised to discover that the rocks weren't really all that hard to avoid. The water was amazingly slow-moving and the stones were well placed, almost as though they'd been set carefully into the river as a barrier of some kind. But a barrier to what? Lucy waited for the current to speed up, but the boat continued to float slowly.

"This is a snap!" exclaimed Wynston.

"Yeah, it's not so bad," Lucy finally said. "I think we're in the clear." Her voice was quieter than usual, but she sounded more like her old self.

Wynston stopped paddling for a second and turned. "About your mother . . ."

Lucy's voice shook a little when she said, "What about her?"

Wynston hesitated when he heard the sadness in Lucy's voice, but then went on. "I'm just not sure I understand."

"What's to understand?"

"Why does it matter so much? I don't have a mother either."

Lucy sighed as she paddled. She'd known they'd have to talk about it at some point. "I guess it feels different. I mean, you see your mother every day, hanging up in the throne room. Your father talks about her, and you've visited her grave. It isn't some big secret for you. But for me . . . well, it is . . . and I'm sick of it. I just want to know."

"I understand." Wynston nodded. "But this seems

185

like a strange way to go about finding out. I mean, why run off to the mountains?"

"There's that song she taught me, and I thought there'd be something here that might tell me about her. I guess I knew all along I probably wouldn't really find her . . . but I wanted to see where she was from, and I thought I might find a clue to where she is. . . ."

"Well, you saw the mountain. Did it help?"

"No, not really. And I asked Steven's mother about her, but she'd never even heard of a Nora in Torrent. And you heard what the chief said—that he didn't know her either. There's only the one town on the mountain, so she must not be here."

"Yeah, that makes sense."

"Wynston, was I crazy to come?"

"Well, if nobody ever said she was . . ." Wynston was afraid to say the word *dead* again. "*Gone* . . . if nobody ever told you that, I guess anything is possible. Though I never thought about it before myself, not like that."

"I never did until recently. But if there's no big secret, why is everyone so mysterious about her?"

"It is a weird kind of a secret. Maybe you're right."

"But then why had nobody ever heard of her back in Torrent?"

"Maybe we need to try another mountain. . . ." They both looked up at the craggy cliffs of the second mountain, which was miles and miles away—a journey of weeks, not days.

"Maybe . . ." Lucy sounded doubtful. "But Steven's mom said they were just gravel and stone. I don't think she'd go there."

"You know, Lucy, you could ask your father."

"Yeah, I guess so . . . but it'll make him so sad. And he's already going to be sad, because now I've lost Rosebud. Sad or really angry . . ." Lucy cringed just thinking about it.

She was about to say something else, but suddenly she yelled out happily instead. Two seconds later, Wynston followed suit, because they could finally see the end of the rocks. There ahead of them was clean, open water and sky. Even Cat poked his head from the bag when Lucy called out, "That's it, that's the last of them! From here on out, I think we're home free!" Jumping up and down in the little boat, Lucy and Wynston were too excited to notice a strange new sound, a rushing roaring noise. Cat noticed the whoosh and splash of the sound, but when he tugged on Lucy's skirt, she only began to sing happily, a silly Thistle song.

In Thistle, where your dad is king,
The dogs all bark and the birds all sing,
But sometimes when it's getting dark,
The dogs all sing and the birds all—

But as they passed the last stone, Wynston cut her off. He leaned eagerly forward to look down at the river and called out, "Here we go—the current should pick up any minute now. Thistle, here we come!" He reached over to touch the surface of the water, but when he did, he pitched suddenly from his seat. He flew into the air and screamed, *"Aaaghghgh!"* Then he disappeared from sight, over the side of the boat.

Lucy stood up with her mouth still open, confused, but only for a heartbeat. Because exactly one second behind Wynston, the entire boat fell. Lucy gasped and clutched for Cat. Down, down, down the boat tumbled, down they all fell, flying from their boat—into the air and over the *waterfall.*

Down they plunged, somersaulting all the way. Down into the cold water of the now fast-moving river. Thankfully, it was a short fall, and Wynston surfaced quickly, coughing and sputtering. He fought the current and swam to the side of the river. He sat in the cattails,

. . . one second behind Wynston, the entire boat fell.

holding fast to the riverbank and shaking the river water from his ears. He plunged his head under the water to look for his friends, but the water was too muddy and grassy, and he couldn't see a thing.

After a while, Lucy's head popped up, and she spit out a mouthful of water. "Are you okay? Where's Cat?" Wynston asked.

"I've got him, I think," said Lucy. "Or, if I don't, I have hold of something else wet and furry. Ugh." She fished Cat from the water and began to swim toward Wynston. Wynston looked down at the bedraggled mess of miserable river-soaked Cat.

Cat sneezed. *"Fishtoo!"*

Once up on the bank, Lucy collapsed onto her stomach. For long minutes she lay like that, one arm curled around Cat, who was (of course) curled once more into a shaking ball. Then Lucy began to weep. Wynston had never seen Lucy cry like this before. He felt afraid, but he reached a hand out to stroke her head.

"Luce?" he said. "It'll all be okay. Rosebud will be okay."

Lucy heaved on the ground awhile longer, but finally she rolled over and wrapped her arms around Wynston.

He could feel her tears on his neck, and they felt strange and soft. But then Lucy pushed away.

"I am so sick and tired of this adventure," Lucy laughed and cried all at once, wiping the tears and spit and grass from her face. "I am so hungry, and I just want to go home!"

"It's okay, Lucy. We'll go home and talk to my father, restock our provisions, and head back up the mountain. We'll get Rosebud back," Wynston said. "And while we're at it, we'll bring Sprout home too. I already miss that darn horse."

"Yeah," said Lucy.

"I don't suppose you have a plan yet?" asked Wynston.

"Nope, but I'm working on it."

"I'll just bet." Wynston began to laugh. He pointed. "You should see yourself!" He guffawed and splashed water at her. "Your hair is just terrible!" He hooted and beat his chest. "Gosh, I feel like I've been whispering ever since I got to Torrent."

Lucy yawped too. *"Aaaaaah!"* she yelled, and then said, "Oh, that does feel good!"

Cat heard their boisterous chatter and uncurled himself in the sun. He began to lick himself dry while

Lucy splashed Wynston back. "Look at yourself, you honorable prince! What's the proper royal etiquette for a waterfall ride?" She splashed harder. "You prince of river mud in your throne of weeds—your father would have a fit if he could see you now!"

"Know what? I don't even care."

"You'll care the minute King Desmond gets hold of you."

Wynston thought seriously for a second. "I don't think so. Really. Look at all the things that have happened. I've run away from home, saved a man from a treacherous stew pot, rescued a widow from eviction, broken into a jail, and fallen down a waterfall. But when I get home, what will my royal father say? He'll be angry because I've ruined my fourth-best jacket, or maybe because I've missed my roast pheasant–carving class. Who cares?" And with that, Wynston climbed up onto the riverbank. He walked downriver about twenty feet, where he could see the boat upturned against a rotting log. "Who really cares at all?"

Lucy followed Wynston to the boat, where he was bent over, tugging at a corner of the capsized craft. She could tell something was happening inside her friend, and she didn't know quite what it was. "Wynston, need any help?"

Wynston looked up, frowned, and smiled just a little. "No, I just *love* turning wet boats over all by myself! It's my most favorite way to spend an afternoon."

"Suit yourself," said Lucy, but she waded back into the river beside him. Together Wynston and Lucy grunted, tugged, and flipped the boat. They scooped it dry with their cupped hands while Lucy finished her song.

In Thistle where your dad is king,
The dogs all bark and the birds all sing,
But sometimes when it's getting dark,
The dogs all sing and the birds all bark.

And sometimes on a summer day,
While the horses moo and the cows say neigh,
I braid my socks and I fold my hair,
Then I go to sleep on a straight-backed chair.

On a Thistle-ish day in a Thistle-y town,
The girls fly up and the boys swim down,
And everyone knows what everything means—
Since things make sense when you sense
    these things.

When she was finished, Wynston said, "That's a pretty good song, Luce, but it doesn't really make any sense."

"Ha. I've had enough of making sense to last a lifetime. Laws and sense and sense and laws! Phooey."

Wynston agreed. "Yeah, phooey."

"I'd like to see you make up a *better* song." Lucy waited, her hands on her hips. She tapped her toe and said, "Not so easy, is it?"

Wynston thought of his own sorry attempt at songwriting when he had been alone at night on the mountain. "All right, you win. How about instead I tell you a funny story?" Lucy agreed, and Wynston told her about his own adventures on the road to the Scratchy Mountains—about Sally crying into her apron, and Willie Wimple in the soup pot, and Persimmon and her braids. Lucy laughed at the funny parts and listened closely to the rest.

When Wynston finished his story, Lucy said, "Wynston, nobody tells a story like you. You're the best!"

And Wynston gave Lucy a funny look in reply. "No, Lucy. You are. You really are." And Lucy knew he meant it.

Since the boat was dry now, they settled Cat back in

his spot beneath the bow and set off down the slow-moving bend of the river. They watched with caution, but now that they'd reached the flat ring of what Lucy had called the mountain's moat, there was really no need for worry. They soon arrived—as if by magic—on the other side of the mountain, not far from the little round home of Willie Wimple. When Wynston saw the house peeking through a stand of trees, he paddled the boat easily to the bank.

Lucy climbed thankfully from the boat and stretched her legs. Cat, drained by his wet adventures, slept noisily in Lucy's bag. But with hours of walking ahead and the sun low in the sky, the adventurers realized they wouldn't be spending the night in Thistle.

"I suppose we'll just have to camp," said Lucy. "Again." She sighed deeply and began to look around for a soft place near the road. But the rumbling in her belly and the muddy-river smell of her dress made her stamp her foot. "Drat, Wynston! I just wanted a pillow and a bowl of soup. Is that too much to ask for?"

"Gosh, no. I was thinking that we should stay overnight at Willie's, if he doesn't mind," Wynston offered. "His house is right over there, through those trees. That's why I stopped the boat here."

"Good, and if he isn't home we can sleep on his porch or something. At the very least we can wash up at his well. From the smell of you, it can only be an improvement." Lucy was cheered by the thought, and she began to skip happily toward an old abandoned barn off in the distance.

Wynston ran to catch up. "Um, Luce—wrong way. It's over here." He pointed to the little round hut.

"Well, how was I supposed to know?" Lucy peered at the round thatched roof. "I mean, that's an awfully funny kind of house."

Wynston just laughed and took her hand. The two walked quickly along the path to Willie's, with Cat whistle-snoring in his bag. In no time at all, they were standing on the doorstep of the little round house. A stream of smoke floated above the chimney, and a thin crack of yellow light shone around the door. Wynston knocked loudly. "Willie, it's me, Wynston! Hey, Willie, I'm back from the mountains. I made it!"

The door swung open and Willie's round face peered out. "Well, if it isn't Wynston. I didn't rightly expect to be seeing you again anytime soon." He glanced at Lucy, who was walking up the steps. "And who's this? A friend?"

"Oh, that's just Lucy." Wynston smiled. "Willie,

meet Lucy. Lucy, this is my friend Willie." Willie and Lucy shook hands.

"Awful late to be out galloping around in the woods," Willie said as he rested his arms on his round belly. "Might you two like some supper and a bed? As I recall, the prince here can eat his own weight in chicken!"

Lucy suddenly thought of something. She piped up from behind Wynston. "Um, we'd love to stay the night, but first, Mr. Willie—"

"Yes, missy?"

"Aren't you originally from Torrent?"

"Why, indeed I am, indeedy I am. Why do you ask?"

"I'm just wondering—" Lucy held her bag closed tightly beside her. "I'm just wondering if you like animals?"

"That's an odd question! Who doesn't like animals?"

"But do you like *all kinds* of animals?"

"Well, to be honest, I'm not much fond of skunks or rats. And rabbits can be something of a problem when they get into my lettuces. But sure! As a general rule, I'm fond of everyone. No reason to be otherwise, hey?"

Lucy sighed in relief and opened her bag. "Then we'd be very grateful for some dinner and a pillow. Ever so grateful. Ever so—" Lucy held a hand to her head. Her eyes crossed for a moment, and she carefully set her bag down on the dirt floor. Cat crawled out and looked up just in time to hear Lucy mutter, "Ever—" Then Cat jumped out of the way and scurried beneath a chair as Lucy fainted.

When she woke up, she was staring into the round, concerned face of Willie Wimple, who kept nervously pinching her cheeks and wiping her forehead with a damp cloth. "I'm fine," she said weakly as she sat up.

Willie reapplied the damp cloth. "Now just you relax, missy—"

Lucy pushed Willie away. "I said I'm fine. Now please leave me be!"

Wynston giggled from somewhere in the room. "*That* sounds like Lucy!"

Lucy looked over at Wynston. "What happened?"

Wynston shrugged. "You just fell down."

"That's ridiculous. I never fall down."

Despite her struggling, Willie leaned over, lifted her into his thick arms, carried her across the room, and set her in a large soft chair. "You fainted, missy, that's all. Nothing to be scared of. I expect you're just hungry and tired."

"I expect I am. Very, very."

"Well, then, come and have some supper. I was just about to have my eight o'clock cake break, but I can warm you up a bit of roast too. Something a little more filling." Willie busied himself in the cupboard while Wynston wrapped Cat in a quilt and Lucy tried to pull some of the snarls from her hair with her fingers.

As he bustled, Willie called out, "Oh, Wynston! Did you happen to get that note to my mother? Did you meet my folks?" He set down a platter of meat and noodles and looked at Wynston. Lucy eyed Wynston carefully as she reached for the gravy boat.

Wynston looked up at Willie. "Willie—I don't know how to say this. Your mother seemed well, but I have to tell you something."

"What's that?"

"It's your father. I'm afraid he's—not there any-more." Wynston picked at the tablecloth.

"Not there? Where'd he run off to? That's not like him at all."

"No. I mean that—well, he's . . . he's—he's passed on, Willie."

"What?"

"Oh, Willie, I'm so sorry."

"Passed on?" repeated Willie, as though he didn't quite understand.

Wynston made a strange face. "Passed on. *Gone.*"

When Lucy heard Wynston utter the word *gone,* she coughed and stomped on his foot heavily. Wynston tried again, in a gentle tone. "He's dead, Willie. I'm so sorry."

Willie sat down quickly on a stool. "Oh my."

Lucy reached out to pat his arm. "I'm so sorry," she began.

"Oh my," repeated Willie. "Well, I suppose it had to come eventually. It's just that I've been gone so long. I guess I forgot things might happen there without me. Goodness, I haven't spoken to my mean old pa in many years. Many, many years. Since long before I left."

"Why not?" asked Lucy gently, sitting on her hands to keep from nibbling at her supper. It didn't seem polite to begin eating, under the circumstances.

"There was a disagreement." Willie rubbed his eyes.

"What did you fight about?" Lucy asked carefully.

Willie rubbed his eyes again. Then he raised his head, but there was a faraway look in his eyes. "You know what?" Willie sighed. "I don't even remember. I think it had something to do with eating dessert before dinner. I always liked my pie first. Father said that was wrong, and I lost my temper and called him a name. I was a brash young man, something of a hothead. Everyone said so."

"Oh, Willie . . ."

"That was the last time we spoke to each other. He never forgave me, and I never apologized. It seems awful silly now, but folks take things seriously in Torrent. There are so many rules about everything and—oh my, that's hard! My poor mother. And to think I don't even know how my poor father passed."

Lucy stood up and walked over to Willie. She kissed the top of his head. "Your mother sounds to be doing well, Willie. And as for your father, I'm sure he knows how you feel."

"That's kind of you to say," said Willie.

"And I don't know if it helps to hear this," added Lucy, "but I don't know a thing about my own mother."

"How's that? Did she pass when you were a young thing?"

"I don't know," said Lucy. "I don't even know if she did pass. I only know a song she sang, and her name, Nora. . . ."

Willie whipped around then, to stare up at Lucy, who stood behind him. "Did you just say Nora?"

Lucy felt a rush, a wind running through her entire body. She walked around the table, trying to collect herself, and then sat back down in her chair. "I said Nora. That was my mother's name, or it *is* my mother's name. Why?"

"Nora," repeated Willie. "Nora. Nora. Sweet Nora. Couldn't be the same one I knew, I don't suppose? You bein' from Thistle and all . . ."

"Actually, it could. It might. See, my mother came from the mountain, though not from Torrent, I don't think, or Steven's mom would have known her."

"Steven's mom?"

"Someone I met on the mountain. She said she didn't know a Nora, and never had. But maybe they just never met?" Lucy looked hopeful.

"Nah, everyone in Torrent knows everyone in Torrent," answered Willie as Lucy's eyes fell again. But Willie continued. "That's not why this lady didn't know Nora. Nora was the best of Torrent, and that's a fact."

"You . . . y-you knew her?" Lucy stammered. She had never been so excited.

"Sure, everyone did. It's a small town."

"Then why . . ."

"Just not everyone knew her as Nora. Only a few of us called her that, assuming we're talking about the same girl."

"She was a goat girl?" asked Lucy.

"She was indeed."

"With red hair?"

"The reddest I ever set eyes on, until I saw yours."

Lucy was so excited she began to feel faint again. "But her name . . ."

"Ah, yes . . . and her name was Eleanor, if you were proper about it, which most are in Torrent. Proper to a fault. Though maybe the rules have changed by now, loosened up a bit?" He raised his eyebrows at Lucy and Wynston, who shook their heads furiously. "I didn't think so. But yes, her proper name was Eleanor. And there was an ordinance."

"An ordinance? But what's wrong with the name Nora?" asked Wynston. "I think it's pretty."

"Of course it is." Willie giggled. "The prettiest name I ever heard, for the prettiest girl that ever herded a goat. Unfortunately, nicknames are not encouraged in Torrent."

"But what about your name?" asked a confused Lucy. "Isn't Willie short for William?"

"Ah . . . ," said Willie, smiling a funny smile. "I can see how you might think that, but no. You see, my own dear mother was something of a radical in her youth, a rabble-rouser. Hard to see now, but she was a wild one in her day. She named me Willie as a kind of joke, because we had a neighbor next door who had a little boy a year older than me, named William. She was thumbing her nose at the law, I'm afraid. You see, there's no law against naming someone a name that's *usually* a nickname. Just against shortening a name. And sometimes it's fun to find out little shortcuts around the rules. . . ."

"So are there certain names you can't use at all?" Lucy asked.

"Nope! Legally, you can name a child anything at all. You could name a little girl, say, Marzipan Almondine, or you could name your little boy Pterodactyl Fishmonger, but then you'd have to say all that mumbo jumbo every time you wanted to call the kids to supper."

Lucy and Wynston tried to digest this. "That's crazy!" said Wynston.

"That's Torrent," said Willie.

Then Lucy woke, as if from a dream, and shook her head. "So you knew my mother?"

"I should say so! I was the biggest boy in the school,

and she was the smallest girl. Somehow we fit together—maybe because neither one of us fit very well in Torrent. Nora always wanted to leave, to find something more. She said she wanted an adventure."

"She did?"

"Yes, indeed. In fact, it wasn't until Nora left town that I had the backbone to leave myself. I always thought I'd find her again, someday. If I came along down the mountain. But I never did."

"That's too bad," said Lucy. "And now she's gone."

"Gone? What happened?"

Lucy shrugged her shoulders. "I wish I could say...."

"Surely your pa knows."

Lucy looked at her hands. "... but I've never asked. I thought she'd gone home, to the mountain. But since we didn't find her in Torrent..."

"Never asked?" Willie looked shocked. His mouth made a round O in his round face, so that he looked a little like a doughnut.

"It sounds crazy now when you say it out loud, but I never asked. Now maybe I will. I think it's time."

Wynston tried to put his arm gently around Lucy's shoulders, but she pushed him away.

Willie was looking sadly at his plate, thinking about

Nora, and his father. Lucy didn't want to disturb him, but finally she broke the silence. "Willie?"

"Yep?" Willie glanced up, and his voice was cheerful, but Lucy saw that his eyes looked sad and tired.

"Do you think I might come and talk to you later, when I know better what happened? Do you think you might be able to tell me some stories about my mother?"

"Of course," said Willie. "It'd be my pleasure. To begin with, she had this song she used to sing. . . ."

And at that, Lucy and Wynston looked up and laughed little somber laughs. Then they all began to sing.

After they'd all sung about the goatherds, Willie stood up. "Listen, kiddles, this has been a big day and an even bigger night. I'm sorry to be such a poor host, but I think I'd best go to bed now. I have some thinking to do. And I'm very, very tired."

"Me too," said Lucy, her thoughts turning to Rosebud.

"Then I'll see you in the morning."

Willie trundled off to sleep, or think, or dream. Wynston and Lucy finished supper, washed their dirty dishes silently, and then curled up by the dying fire, wrapped in soft blankets for the first time all week. They turned their backs to each other and tunneled into their beds. Wynston thought about his father, and about what it means to be a king. Lucy, who had too much to think about, fell straight to sleep.

"G'night, Lucy," said Wynston.

"Zzzzzzz," said Lucy in reply.

Cat snuggled close.

HEADING HOME, AND ARRIVING

ONE ESPECIALLY bright sunbeam wriggled its way around the heavy curtain and woke Lucy the next morning. She yawned and stretched happily in the warmth of the cottage, and then she elbowed Wynston. "Are you up yet?" She jabbed a little harder and poked him in the ear. "Hey, Wynston, are you awake? Wynston?"

In answer, Wynston snorted and rolled over onto Cat, who gave an enormous *"Owrfff,"* which woke everyone up entirely. Willie pattered in, flustered, from his bedroom. "My stars! What is it now? What, which, when, where, Wynston?"

Lucy, Wynston, and Cat all looked up at Willie, tousled and half asleep. Wynston rubbed his eyes in apology. "Nothing. Sorry to wake you, Willie."

"Oh, it's fine, fine, fine. I should be getting up now, anyway. With all the excitement of last night, I'm afraid I overslept." Willie yawned and tugged at his nightcap, which slid from his head onto the floor. Cat crawled inside it and promptly went back to sleep. "There's not much for breakfast, I'm afraid, since I didn't know I'd be having company. We'll have to make do with ham and eggs and fried potatoes and pie—and coffee, of course. How does that suit you?"

This sounded like a feast to Lucy and Wynston, who nodded their heads agreeably and went out to the well to wash up. They combed their hair and shook the acorns and twigs from their shoes. When they stepped back inside the cottage, heaping plates awaited them. After a hearty meal, Lucy wiped a smear of yolk from the corner of her mouth and said, "Willie, you've been such a wonderful host. We're entirely grateful, but we're eager to get home now."

"Of course you are, of course. I must say, I think I'm ready to head for home myself."

"But this *is* your home," said Lucy.

Willie scratched his belly thoughtfully. "I suppose that depends on your definition of home."

"Then—you mean home to your mother? Back up

the mountain to Torrent?" Wynston asked with a grimace.

Willie just sighed. "I did some heavy thinking last night. Couldn't sleep for all the thoughts in my noodle. I guess I always knew this day would come. I left so many years back, but home is home is home, and a widowed mother is a widowed mother. It's bad enough I missed my pa, but I hate to think—" He knitted his brow.

"If you're really going back," said Lucy, "can you do something for me? Something very important?"

"Anything!" answered Willie. "I owe Wynston here a great deal, for a certain incident concerning a soup pot, among other things. I'd love to repay the favor."

"It would be just wonderful if you could check in on my little cow, Rosebud. She's up there somewhere, probably with the chief or the mayor. If you could just make sure she's taken care of until I can get back."

"Why, of course!"

"Sprout too?" Wynston added.

"Well, I'd have fed him some sugar the minute I saw him, even without you asking." Willie grinned.

"Before we leave, Willie, do you mind if I ask why you ran off in the first place?" asked Lucy. "It's something I'm curious about . . . people running away."

"Oh—people run away for very different reasons, Lucy."

"Still, I'd like to hear the story."

"It was all so long ago, and it seems awfully silly now."

"What seems silly?" asked Lucy.

"Well—you were there such a short time that I don't suppose you'd have noticed, but Torrent's different from Thistle. It's what we Torrentians call a *very civilized place.*"

"We noticed," chorused Lucy and Wynston.

"Unfortunately, it was a little too civilized for big, bumbling old me. I was always bumping into things: into fences and laws and mailmen and other people's feelings. I was always spilling the milk, breaking the teapot, and kicking the cobblestones loose. One time I accidentally glued myself to a chair!"

Lucy tried not to laugh at the thought. She pulled her collar up over her nose.

"Oh no, go ahead and laugh." Willie smiled as he remembered. "I was a disaster. I don't know if it was me or the town itself, but I just never seemed to fit in to Torrent. After my father and I stopped speaking, it seemed even worse. Then one day, I broke our front door." Willie sighed. "Which sounds like a little problem to people who grew up in a place with all kinds of doors. But in Torrent, all the doors are alike. They're very old, and protected by a historical decree. You aren't allowed to have any other kind of door. But to get a new one requires what's called archival doormanship, and takes years."

"That sounds silly," said Lucy. "It's just a door."

"You'd think that," said Willie, "but in Torrent, things are as they are. And my poor mother was mortified to live that way, with no door, people peering in at all hours, the room getting wet each evening. She never said a word to me, but I could tell she was ashamed. And shame is a terrible thing. Bad to feel, and worse to cause. So I set off on my own."

"I'm awful glad you did," said Wynston.

"Me too!" agreed Willie. "I've seen so much, and done so many wonderful things. But maybe it's time for me to get used to the rules now. With my old pa gone, my mother will need help around the house. I've missed her, and the green misty trees, and the view of the valley in the clear noon sky." He took a deep breath. "Torrent is, all in all, very pretty. Maybe I'll run for mayor and give Callow a little competition. If I win I can always widen the streets and nail down the cobblestones." Willie winked as he said this, patting his ample belly.

Lucy and Wynston laughed. They gave Willie enormous hugs and wished him luck. Then they began the journey home along the familiar road to Thistle, kicking a pinecone back and forth between them as they walked.

Wynston finally broke the silence and said slowly, "You're really going back?"

"First chance I get!"

"For Rosebud, or for your mother?"

"That'll depend."

"On what?"

"On Papa, I think. On the truth, whatever it is."

"Oh," said Wynston, who was happy Lucy felt better, and scared for what she might find out. He had a feeling. . . .

"Listen, Wynston. As much as I hate to admit it, you were right. Leaving Rosebud was the only choice. This one time you were right." Lucy walked even faster than usual, which was pretty fast.

Wynston hurried to keep up. He grabbed Lucy's arm to slow her down. "Wait—what did you just say?"

Lucy pulled her arm free and scowled a little scowl. "Nothing! I didn't say anything."

"Yes, you did. You just said—"

"Oh, fine. I said you were right. Are you happy? You

were right, right, right, okay? And while I'm at it . . . you were right to follow me up the mountain too." Lucy walked ahead very quickly. "Not because I couldn't have saved myself, but because it was better to do it together."

"Really?" asked Wynston.

"Yeah, really," said Lucy.

"It's nice . . . working on things together. I mean, I never would have thought up a plan to save Cat, or jumped into the jail like that. But it did feel really nice to pull you up. It felt nice to help."

"I'm glad," said Lucy. "I was lucky you came along. I know I'm usually kind of bossy, and I like to take care of myself. But it was nice, this time, to have someone else to help me out a little. And besides . . ."

"Besides?"

"Besides . . . I missed you . . . kind of a lot," Lucy said as she sped down the road.

"Thanks, Lucy!" Wynston called after her. "I mean it, thanks!" He laughed out loud.

Lucy broke into a run. She yelled back at him over her shoulder, "Just don't get used to it, okay? I don't expect I'll have to say that again for, oh—I don't know—twenty-eight years at least!"

Then Wynston chased her as fast and as far as he

214

could, calling after her. Finally they both raced into the main square of Thistle, where they collapsed, panting and happy.

Inside the castle, King Desmond sat at the kitchen table, worriedly licking spice-cake batter from a large spoon. Masha bustled around him, patting his head and stroking his arm from time to time. She poured him a glass of buttermilk but then drank it herself, fretting all the while. The king didn't even notice. He just stared at his spoon and continued to lick long after the batter was gone, while Masha peeled every carrot in the larder for no particular reason.

Then the king threw his spoon across the room. "Peacock pie and whisker stew! Do you think I've been too hard on the boy, Masha? Do you think this is my fault, like his aunt says?"

Masha jabbed a fork pointlessly into a pumpkin and shook her head so hard that her bun came loose. "No sir, certainly not. Wynston's a dear boy, but eventually he was bound to turn into a shooting star. It wouldn't be natural if he behaved all the time. Boys have to grow, like pole beans and mushrooms and everything else.

215

Why, I remember another young prince who built himself a magic balloon and planned to sail off over the Green Ocean with only his blind hunting dog for company!"

The king laughed in spite of himself. "I'd forgotten all about that. I never did get the darn thing off the ground." He pouted again. "But that was entirely different! I built that balloon in the name of progress, as a princely duty. I was going to discover something, and besides, I was just a boy!"

Masha only leaned into the vegetable bin, looking for something else to peel. She came out with a large purple turnip. "Indeed? As I recall, you were precisely the age that Prince Wynston is now. And the prince certainly had his reasons for tearing off into the mountains—not bad reasons neither. He went in search of Lucy, or so her sister told the assistant to the assistant scullery maid, Teeny. I sent her by the dairy, to look for the prince. He's rescuing a damsel in distress, and that's a princely sort of thing, I'd say." She looked up from her turnip. "Wouldn't you agree?"

The king made a *harumph* noise, but he didn't try to argue. Instead, he twisted his napkin into the shape of a lopsided hunting dog. He tilted his head to one side and peered at the napkin, as though wondering if it might bark. "It's been hard these past few days, Masha. I won't lie to you. Wynston's all I've got, and I'm so muddled in my noggin that I can't tell if he needs a gigantic hug or an enormous wallop. Lavinia, poor thing, has taken to her bed with a bottle of floofleberry schnapps. She's been weeping since Wynston left. Nonstop."

Masha clucked, "Poor thing. I should take her a bit of cake."

"And all the business with the Queening has me over a barrel as well! I hate to admit it, but Lucy wasn't far off about the twit-nits. The only princesses on the market these days are—well, a little daft. I'll be darned if I'll marry my only son off to a girl with the brain of a feather duster." The king sighed three times deeply. "It does seem that Lucy is the lady for my son, but laws are laws. My poor dead grandfather, King Ponciferous III, would turn in his grave to hear of a common queen in the throne room, a milkmaid monarch! Masha, what can I do?"

"Sir, I'm just a simple cook—a servant in this house. All I'm good for is roasting and baking and saucing and stuffing and peeling and grinding and mending and cleaning and washing and overseeing the staff and plan-ning the meals and organizing the royal festivities and such. I wouldn't think to tell a king how to handle his son, but I'll say this—Wynston is a good boy, and you're a wise king, and Miss Lucy is always welcome in my kitchen, wherever my kitchen may be."

Then the timer dinged on the stove, and Masha put on her oven mitts. The king scratched his beard thoughtfully as he repeated her last sentence slowly under his breath. "Wherever your kitchen may be?"

Now that they were almost home, Lucy and Wynston walked slowly. They practically trudged along the road to the castle, dreading what might meet them at the door. Wynston was afraid of his father, because he knew he had a lot of explaining to do. He tried to think of the best way to answer for the loss of Sprout and the bad public relations with the mayor of Torrent. He thought and thought, and came up with absolutely nothing.

Meanwhile, Lucy thought about Rosebud, still on top of the mountain, but most of all she thought about her father and her mother. She tried to think about the best way to ask a hard question. She walked slower and slower until she found herself standing still. She sat down and picked at the grass beside her. She pulled Cat from the bag. He woke up, sneezed, and then went back

They practically trudged along the road to the castle . . .

to sleep on the sunny patch of grass. Lucy started thread-ing the grass blades and the clover together, to make a necklace. And she sang, but more quietly than usual.

> *I thought I knew some things, but then*
> *I learned I knew them wrong, and when*
> *I found I'd made a giant mess,*
> *I made another, more or less.*

Wynston plopped down beside her and looked up at the castle looming above them.

"Almost home, Luce. It's funny to realize that we've only been gone a few days. It feels like we've been on the mountain forever."

"Uh-huh."

Wynston leaned back and stretched out on the ground, chewing on an extra-long blade of grass. "Say, Luce, I've been thinking—"

"That's unusual."

Wynston ignored her snark and tried again. "No, seriously. I've been thinking—and I think maybe we should get married."

Lucy sucked in a deep breath and stopped braiding the clover stems. Wynston examined his shoes, waiting to see what she'd say. Then Lucy looked over and stared down at Wynston until Wynston stared back up at her. Neither of them spoke for what felt like hours. Finally Wynston blinked.

"I win," said Lucy, and went back to picking grass.

"No, Lucy. I really mean this." Wynston sat up and took her hand, but she snatched it away. He grabbed for it again and held it tightly this time. "Stop playing with the grass and listen to me, Lucy!"

She tried to pull her hand away. "Ow, that hurts!"

Wynston let go. "Sorry, I didn't mean to do that. Just, please listen—please?" He took a deep breath. "I don't want things to be like they were before we ran away. I don't want all of that royal mess, all those lessons and meetings and fittings and sizings and silly meals that take so long that I fall asleep in my dessert. I don't want to go back to the castle after all the things we saw on the mountain, and marry some silly girl I don't even know. I don't want to follow rules just to follow rules . . . not anymore."

Lucy stood up and brushed off her skirt. She tried to fit the clover necklace over her head, but it was too small and it sat on her curls instead. She pulled off the accidental crown and tossed it at Wynston. "This is all the crown I'll ever need, you—you prince!" She scooped Cat into the bag and headed back to the road. Wynston ran after her.

"Wait, Lucy, listen to me!"

Lucy turned and glared at him. "No! I do not want to marry anyone just yet, and I do not want to go breaking any more laws. You may be just learning to break the rules, but it's nothing new for me. All the rule breaking did was cause me to lose Rosebud. Besides, I do not especially care to live in that cold castle anyway!"

Wynston snapped back. "Why do you have to be so darn difficult? What if you don't have to marry me *yet*, and what if there aren't any laws broken? What about that?" Wynston kneeled down on one knee. "I'm so serious, Lucy. I really mean it. You're my best friend. I don't want to sound all squooshy and wooshy and weird, but I—I don't want to miss any more Sundays in the berry patch because I'm looking for a silly princess who doesn't go berrying because she's afraid to scuff her shoes. Will you marry me *someday*, Lucy? Will you marry me if we don't have to break any laws—please?"

Lucy crossed her arms. "Oh, get up, already! You're embarrassing me."

"Please?"

"Can Cat come with me?"

Wynston smiled. "Of course."

"And you'll help me rescue Rosebud?"

"Yes, of course. I already promised."

"Pinky swear?"

Wynston held out his pinky.

"Well then, I suppose I will marry you *someday*, in about eleven or twelve years—if you don't get any funnier-looking than you are now, and if you stop doing silly things like this!" She turned and walked off. Wynston scrambled to his feet and ran after her.

"So then, we're engaged?"

"If that's what you want to call it. Now hurry up!"

As Lucy and Wynston were trooping up the castle steps, King Desmond was pacing back and forth in his throne room and muttering to Lucy's father, who was sitting nervously on the king's throne. It was the first time he'd set foot in a castle, much less sat on a throne.

"If we shift the—and move the—then the—will be understandably—oh my goodness!" fretted the king. Every now and then he ran to the table beside the throne to consult a very large and dusty book that smelled like old shoes. He was so lost in his important royal distractions that he didn't notice when Wynston and Lucy knocked at the door. Lucy's father just pointed when Wynston walked carefully and quietly into the room. Lucy tiptoed behind him and squeezed her hands together behind her back. Wynston cleared his throat and the king whirled around.

"Wynston!" He ran toward his son, his purple robe flying behind him in a most undignified manner. His crown fell off his head as he grabbed Wynston and smothered him in a bear hug. "My son, oh, my son! You're home safe at last. Oh my goodness, boy, wherever did you go? We've been dreadfully worried."

Lucy's father eased himself down from the tall throne, opened his arms, and Lucy ran into them.

Wynston was confused by the warm reception. He'd been expecting a different sort of welcome. "We just went—or rather, I just went to find Lucy and then we—"

Lucy pulled herself from her father's lap to try and help explain, but King Desmond waved his hand at both of them.

"No matter, son, no matter. We have more important things to discuss. The time has come to settle this marriage business. I'll have no more mincing about. I've talked with Princess Halcyon and her family, and I think—"

Now it was Wynston's turn to wave his hand. He spoke very slowly and firmly, to keep from sounding like a little boy. "No, Dad. I'm not talking with Halcyon any more, and I'm not interviewing any other princesses either." Wynston took the deepest breath of his life. "I don't need to find a suitable princess because I don't plan to be king. Not ever." He stopped speaking and looked at Lucy and King Desmond. He waited for the shock to register in both of their faces. But that wasn't quite what happened. King Desmond smiled ever so slightly, and Lucy spoke.

She planted both hands on her hips and said, "Don't be a numbskull, you numbskull! That's the most ridiculous thing I've ever heard. If I knew that was your plan from the beginning, I'd never have agreed."

"Why is it ridiculous? Torrent doesn't have a king—so why do we need one in Thistle? I'll be a mayor instead, and then we don't have to break any laws."

Lucy looked like she'd been drinking sour milk. "Oh, and things run so smoothly in Torrent? Maybe *we'll* become *very civilized* too, and you can wear a stupid hat or poke poor defenseless animals with spoons. No thanks, Wynston. The deal is *off*!"

Wynston's face fell. He turned to look at his father

but was surprised to find that King Desmond did not look shocked or angry or hurt. In fact, King Desmond looked amused.

"And why don't you want to be king, my boy? Not good enough for you? Or maybe you're afraid of the job," he teased. He adjusted his crown with one hand and stroked his chin with the other. "I can see why you'd be frightened. I've set the bar rather high—left some mighty big shoes to fill!"

"No, that isn't it at all, though of course you're a wonderful king and all that! It's just that— Dad, I'm going to marry Lucy and you can't stop me. I don't care what you discussed with Halcyon. I'm sorry if I'm making you look bad, but you'll just have to tell her I've changed my mind. Lucy and I don't want to break any laws, so I thought if I weren't king—"

The king rapped Wynston sharply on the head. "That's enough of that. What I was going to say, before I was so rudely interrupted, is that I've talked to Princess Halcyon and her family—and I've explained that there isn't going to be a wedding."

Wynston stood with his mouth hanging open, feeling a little foolish. Lucy tried not to giggle at him while the king continued, "Furthermore, I have examined all of the laws and bylaws concerning royal marriages, and concerning the royal residence—"

"The royal residence?"

"Yes, this castle . . . that's what they call it in that book over there." He pointed to the funny, smelly old tome and continued, "And I have discovered that while Lucy may not live in the royal residence—"

"The royal residence?"

"Stop saying that! I have discovered that while Lucy may not live here, there is no law that requires that the king himself live in the castle."

"What do you mean? Castles are where kings live."

The king groaned. "My boy! Must you cut me off at every turn? Think outside the tiny box, you buffoon! Just because kings have always lived in castles doesn't mean they *must* live in castles. In fact, there's no law about it at all. *This*, my boy, is what we call a loophole!"

At this, King Desmond leaned over and pulled a twig triumphantly from Wynston's hair. "From the looks of you, your bed last night was a far cry from the royal chambers, and you seem to have survived it. Besides, the world is changing. Maybe a shake-up will do us all some good. Therefore, I have decided to move it all—the thrones, the books, the crowns, and the rubies—to a

more suitable location." When King Desmond said the word *suitable*, he snickered to himself.

"Suitable?" echoed Wynston.

"Well, suitable for a scamp who can't seem to stay put. Suitable for a prince who prefers the company of milkmaids to the—"

"The dairy!" Lucy cried out. "You can come to live at the dairy, Wynston! Right, Dad?" Her father smiled and nodded.

The king grinned from ear to ear. "That's it, my girl! That's it exactly! Wynston, my boy, it seems that Lucy's a little quicker than you."

Lucy smirked as the king continued to advise his son. "I think that perhaps you'd better marry her. A complicated kingdom like this one requires at least one clever monarch." He laughed at his own joke.

"But what will we do with all the cows if we move the rubies into the barn?" asked a surprised and confused Wynston.

The king paused and stroked his chin again. "Hmmm. I hadn't thought of that, but I've always liked animals. I don't believe there's any law against cows in the royal estate, just commoners. Your aunt could use a new challenge— she's become rather too fond of floofleberry schnapps in your absence. And just think! I won't be expected to wear my best clothes for milking, so I'll be able to dribble and drabble to my heart's delight. Prickly prune gravy, here I come—" He left the throne room, whistling cheerfully to himself.

At the door, he turned and paused, then called back over his shoulder to Lucy and Wynston, "And, Wynston, here's a good thing to know, if you're going to be king. No good comes of breaking laws, but there are usually a few wonderful ways to bend them!"

(AFTER, AND AFTER THAT)

THE NEXT day Lucy wandered out to the barn. She took Cat with her, thinking that after his wet adventures he'd like the warmth and the smell of the hay on the floor. Together they sat. Lucy watched Cat, who watched Lucy's papa as he milked. Lucy made sure that when Cat scrambled in the hay, she knew just where he was at all times. She brought a variety of snacks in her pockets (carrots and almonds and some cheese too), since she still hadn't figured out what he liked to eat. But Cat chewed on a bit of hay and then pounced on a centipede instead. Lucy made a face as he chomped on the wiggling legs, but she kept him close, and quiet. She watched him explore. After a few minutes, she spoke slowly. "Papa?"

"Yep?"

"Papa, can I ask you something?"

"Yes, Lucy. But can you hold Lilac's tail for a minute so I can concentrate?" He handed Lucy the cow's tail.

Lucy took a deep breath. "I don't know any other way to say this, and I know it makes you sad to think about it . . . but I need to know about Mama." She heard her father suck in his breath quickly. His face tightened.

"What do you want to know?"

"Well, mostly, I want to know where she is."

"Where she is?" Lucy's father didn't turn his head, and Lucy listened for a minute to the sound of milk pinging into the bucket. "What do you mean?"

Lucy felt her voice rise, grow louder. "I want to know where Mama went when she left us!"

Still he didn't turn his head. "Lucy, she's . . . *gone.*"

There was a beat of silence before Lucy spoke next, like the calm before a storm cloud breaks. "Gone?" She repeated the word she'd grown to hate. "Gone?"

He continued milking. "Yes, Lucy. Gone."

Suddenly Lucy was furious and sad and confused all at the same time. She hated that word. That word meant nothing. She didn't care anymore about making her father unhappy. She thought about Rosebud, stranded on the mountain, and about all the dreadful things that might have happened to her in Torrent. Lucy wasn't sorry she'd had her adventure. But all in a huge rush, she understood for the first time that her father owed her this, the story of her mother. For the first time in her life, she yelled at her papa.

"Papa!" she said sharply to his back. "Papa, look at me! *Talk* to me!" He turned at last. "Don't you understand? All you've ever said was *gone*! What does *gone* mean? My mother means nothing more than that word. No face, no stories. She's an empty place, *gone*."

"Lucy . . ."

"*No!* I need you to use a different word, a word that means something. What happened, Papa? What happened to her?" She was crying now, hard as nails. "Why did she leave me?"

"Oh, Lucy . . ." Her father reached out to hold her, but she pulled away. "Do I really need to say it?"

Slowly Lucy stopped shaking, and her tears rolled silently down as she spoke in a still, small voice. "Say the word, Papa. Say it!"

"Lucy, your mother is . . . dead." The word fell like the first drop in a metal tub. And Lucy stood stone still.

Then Lucy picked up Cat, who was trying to climb a rickety ladder, and she snuggled her wet face in his fur.

"How did she die?" Lucy's voice shook ever so slightly.

"She . . ." Lucy's father rose from his milking stool and turned to face her. His eyes were full of tears. "She—Nora—was the kindest, most lovely person that ever lived, Lucy. Your mother was so beautiful. We were so happy. And then there was a storm." The word echoed in the barn, and the air felt very still.

"A storm?"

Lucy's father knelt in front of her and took her hands. "Are you certain you want to hear this? It isn't a nice story. It was always too hard to talk about, and I didn't want to scare you. Are you sure you're ready?"

"I'm sure," said Lucy. And she was. The word *storm* felt good to her. It was something she needed, something to hold on to. She could picture a *storm*, in a way she'd never been able to picture *gone*. Trees and wind and rain and loud crashing noises. One word, just one, and already Lucy could begin to feel the truth—hard and terrible, but real. How could something so frightening make her feel . . . better?

Lucy's father spoke in a stony voice, as though he were practicing a speech. "There was a terrible storm. Your mother had been hanging laundry beside the house all afternoon on a wire strung between two trees. I remember it like yesterday."

Tears began to well up in his eyes. "It was a pretty day, and you were asleep in a basket beneath the pear tree. You liked to watch the clothes flap in the wind, so she always took you with her. That day . . . you had sung yourself to sleep. You had just learned to sing and we were so proud. . . ."

"I was there?"

"You were sleeping. Your mother had always hated rain. She said it reminded her of her home on the mountain. But the storm rolled in so fast that there wasn't time to take the laundry down. Your mother ran to fetch you from the basket, where you were sleeping soundly, despite the rain. But she tripped on a root and fell beside one of the trees. As she fell, a tremendous bolt of lightning struck the tree. That awful pear tree!"

"Struck her?"

"It killed her instantly."

Lucy put one hand to her mouth. Tears filled her eyes, and she took a minute to think about things. But then she wondered something, and she couldn't help but ask. "How do you know, Papa . . . how do you know it killed her instantly? That it happened just like that?"

"Because—" Lucy's father choked as he began to weep. "Because—I watched it through the window. I saw it all—just there." He pointed across the yard to a window.

"Oh, Papa!"

"And I should have gone out into the rain with her, to help her. I would have. If I had known you were out there—if I had known what she was doing. She hated the rain so. But I didn't realize until it was too late. I saw her reach for your basket, and there was a sound—an awful sound. Oh, Lucy . . ."

"Oh, Papa, I'm so sorry."

"I know, sweet girl. I know."

Lucy took a minute to think. "Papa, is there a . . . does she have a grave? Where I could visit her?"

Lucy's father took her hand, pulled her into his lap. "I'm afraid not. You see, the lightning started a fire, and it burned so fast. There was nothing . . . nothing left for us to bury." He choked on the terrible words.

"I'm so sorry, Papa."

"No, Lucy. Please don't ever feel sorry. It's me who

feels sorry . . . that I didn't tell you sooner. You deserved the truth. Even if I couldn't give you your mama, I could've given you the truth."

"Oh, Papa." As sad as Lucy felt on the inside, she felt so much worse for her father. And she understood everything in that moment. His awful silence. Why he stared sadly at his feet when he heard the name Nora.

"It was as if she had just vanished. Like she'd never been. There was just an empty space and that awful burnt tree. That horrible tree. I dug up the roots. I chopped it up and then I burned it. All of it."

"Oh, Papa . . ."

"Lucy, I hate pears. But you know, Lucy . . . even without your mother, you've grown up so well, and I'm so proud of you."

"Truly?"

"Of course. Why, just look at you, with Cat, almost like a mother yourself!"

She picked Cat up and snuggled him hard. "Thank you, Papa."

And her papa reached out and hugged Lucy just as hard.

"Now, come with me. I have something to show you.

But first let's find your sister. She needs to know these things too."

"But Sally says she doesn't want to know about Mama. Sally says it's best to keep quiet."

Lucy's papa sighed. "Your sister is a very good girl, Lucy. She does as she's told, and listens carefully. But maybe, this time, she's listened a little too carefully to her sad papa. I think, deep down, Sally will want to know too. Don't you?"

Lucy thought about this and then nodded in agreement. So she picked up Cat and tore off to the house, calling her sister's name loudly. When Lucy stepped inside, Sally looked up from where she was reading quietly in a chair. "What is it, Lucy? What could possibly be worthy of such a hullabaloo?"

But under the circumstances, even Sally's persnickety speech couldn't keep Lucy's face from shining. "Oh, Sally, it's *Mama*. I know you said you didn't want to know, but Papa is telling us about *Mama*!"

At that, Sally dropped her book and didn't even bother to pick it up. The confusion and happiness in her eyes matched the glow on Lucy's face. "Truly? Truly?"

And then Lucy's father stepped inside. And from

inside the closet, from the top tiny shelf, above the coats and aprons, he took a box, a carved wooden box. He beckoned Lucy and Sally into the kitchen and, choking back tears, set the box on the kitchen table. "You both should have seen this long ago. Your mother brought it with her from the mountain. And now it belongs to you girls."

Lucy lifted the lid. From inside the box, she picked up a hand mirror. It was blue, and intricately carved with odd letters and flowers. Tiny goats peered out from the carvings, and the old mirror that was set in the center was a little clouded. But Lucy could see her face, her own red hair, and her own blue eyes smiling back at her. She smiled.

Then her papa turned her hand over. At first Lucy thought that there might be another mirror on the back, but there wasn't. It was a painting, a lifelike portrait of another face, with another pair of smiling blue eyes. Another halo of red curls. A face almost identical to her own. Lucy's hand shook, but she didn't drop the handle. She held her mother and, for a minute, felt her mother holding her too.

It was a painting, a lifelike portrait of another face . . .

And in case you are asking yourself, *But what about Rosebud?* I'll set your mind at ease. There was, a few weeks later, another voyage up the mountain. A plan was hatched, and bags were packed. But this time Lucy and Wynston zipped up the mountain in a shiny green boat, wearing sturdier boots and singing excitedly. Masha made sure there were plenty of meat pies to go around.

Cat stayed home in the barn, safe and dry.

And though I will not reveal the details of that adventure, because this story has nearly reached its end . . . I will assure you that Rosebud was (after some searching) discovered at the home of Mayor Callow, wearing a bright yellow ribbon. And I will further inform you that Sprout was found in the same location, though without such colorful adornment.

I will also say that when the party arrived, they found that Willie had indeed made it home, slowly, and not without mishap. He was happy to be there among the misty fields, heavy branches, and narrow, wet streets. His mother was very pleased to have him home, even though he continued to bump into things, causing a variety of interesting disasters.

But that . . . is a story all its own.

Darling reader, gentle friend,
Doors must shut and days must end.
All things start, and stop, and then,
They get started up again.

Winter turns to spring and clover.
Just like that, this book is over.
So . . . for now, a hug and kissle,
From your many friends in Thistle.

ACKNOWLEDGMENTS

My deepest thanks . . .

To Chris Poma, who suggested I begin writing this book, and Marvin and Dorothy Bell, who urged me to finish.

To Lisa Findlay, Tina Wexler, and Mallory Loehr, who made this experience a fairy tale all its own.

To Gary Blankenburg and Richard Jackson, who suggested (when I was young enough to believe them) that I *might* someday be a *real* writer.

To Thisbe Nissen, Julianna Baggott, and Elizabeth Lenhard, who offered sound advice and cheerful chatter.

To Sonya Naumann and Jeff Skinner, who aided and abetted.

To Susan Gray, with whom I first wandered the Bewilderness.

To my parents—Mom, Dad, Steve, and Cheryl—who built a house of stories. And to Henry, Emma, and Roy, who lived in that house with me.

To the University of Iowa, which granted me a James Michener–Paul Engle Fellowship and the luxury of time to write.

And finally, to the authors I've loved best and the people who led me to them: C. S. Lewis and Kate Hamill, W. B. Yeats and Steve Snyder, James Thurber and Steve Gettinger, Maurice Sendak and Judy Goldstein. Also Roald Dahl, Susan Cooper, Joan Aiken, P. L. Travers, Betty MacDonald, L. Frank Baum, Lewis Carroll, Norton Juster, Edward Eager, E. Nesbit, and the generous librarians of the Enoch Pratt Free Library, who were my babysitters, friends, and teachers for many years.

I owe you all a great deal.

If you had a magic wall that could take you to *any* place and *any* time, where would you go?

Turn the page for a sneak peek at
Laurel Snyder's next book, *Any Which Wall*!

If the Key Fits

"Wow," said Henry, staring up.

Everyone agreed: the wall *was* "wow." It looked like something from another place and time, ancient and mysterious, leaning over them. They just stood. Gaping. Up.

"It's so big," said Roy after a while. "What do you think it *was*? I mean, what did it start out as, back when it was built?"

"A castle!" Emma answered right away with absolute certainty. "A big giant castle. For when people needed to hide from Indians and wolves and for olden-time princesses to stay in when they visited Iowa."

"Mmmmm. More likely a farmhouse," said Susan. "I don't think there are a lot of castles in Iowa, Em—"

"Actually, Susan," said Roy, "I don't think a farmhouse makes any more sense than a castle. It's too huge for a house. Plus, if it *were* part of a house, it'd have some windows in it, right? And maybe a door?"

They all looked up and agreed that the wall didn't have any windows in it, or doors either. Susan frowned.

"Maybe it was a really enormous barn?" Roy guessed. "But it doesn't matter much. The big question is, what can we do with it?"

The others agreed. Clearly, something so interesting and rare needed to be put to good use.

"I guess it could be a kind of fort," said Susan at last, "if we leaned some branches against it, maybe. But they'd have to be really long branches."

"And where would we get the branches from?" asked Roy, thinking practically. "Drag them from town?"

"Who cares!" said Henry impatiently. "We can figure out what to do with it later. In the meantime, we should claim it."

"Claim it?" asked Emma.

"Yeah, Em. Like when someone finds a planet or walks on the moon or something. Or back in pioneer days, when they staked out homesteads in the Wild West. It's *our* wall now. We found it, and we need to claim it before someone else does. Right, Roy?"

"We can if you want to." Roy nodded thoughtfully.

"Although *technically* it belongs to whoever owns this field."

Henry ignored this comment. Roy was his best friend and always had been, but sometimes it was necessary to ignore Roy in the name of fun. Henry wished his friend could understand that "technically" didn't always matter.

"But what are we going to claim it *with*?" Henry asked. "We should have a flag or a sign or something, a way to let people know that it's *our* wall. What have you guys got?"

They all emptied their pockets.

Henry had half a pack of very pungent bubble gum (the same gum that had left his hair a sticky mess), a handful of change, a crumpled dollar bill, the cell phone his mother made him carry, and a red rubber ball. Emma found one of the green handlebar tassels from her new bike (already pulled loose), a smiling-tooth sticker from the dentist's office, and another crumpled dollar bill. Susan found a tube of sparkle lip gloss, ten dollars (emergency money), a cell phone nobody ever had to remind her to carry, and a barrette. Roy found a funny-looking rock, a compass, and a mouse skull, which is not nearly as gross as it sounds. He pulled the skull out last, and it gleamed fragile and white in his hand.

"I don't know how we can make a sign or a flag with any of this stuff," said Henry, "but *that*"—he pointed at the skull—"gives me another idea. You know what would be awesome?" The others did not know, so Henry told them. "We should have some kind of ceremony. Make a sacrifice and say a prayer of thanks, like when shipwrecked people find a desert island. To thank the spirits of the field, or whatever, for letting us find the wall." Henry was excited. This would involve digging, jumping around, and make-believe: three of his favorite things.

Henry began to make a chanting noise that sounded like "Oh-ee-oh-ee," and bowed down to the wall. After a while, he turned and looked back at the others, wondering why nobody else had joined in his wordless song. They were all just watching him.

"A sacrifice?" Emma looked nervous.

Henry stopped chanting and sighed. "I don't mean a scary kind of sacrifice," he explained. "I mean a fun sacrifice."

"If we're going to do a sacrifice, we should do it right," said Susan. "A sacrifice should mean giving up something more than an old piece of bone." She eyed the skull with distaste. "A sacrifice should be something you care about. Something you want to keep. That's the *definition* of sacrifice, isn't it? That way, the spirits will know we're serious."

The others stared at her when she said the word "spirits." This didn't sound like the Susan they'd gotten used to over the last year, the Susan who ignored them and sometimes made fun of their games. This seemed more like the old Susan, and though they were delighted to welcome her return, they were all a little shocked.

She noticed them staring and stared right back, in a bug-eyed sort of way. "What?" she said. "I just mean—you know, if there *are* spirits."

Roy prodded her. "So, you think we need to give up something that matters to us?"

Susan nodded.

"Like . . . your cell phone?" asked Roy with a sneaky smile.

"Yeah," said Henry, smirking. "You sure do like *that*."

"No way," said Susan, putting it back in her pocket immediately. "Absolutely not. Mom and Dad would kill me."

"What about the money, then?" asked Emma.

Of all the things they were carrying with them, their money did seem like the only thing they had worth giving up, besides their two cell phones, which—everyone had to admit—they'd get skinned alive if they lost. It didn't seem likely that the spirits of the field would want a plastic tassel or some gum, so while Roy dug a hole at the base of the wall, Susan collected Emma and Henry's dollars.

"On second thought," Susan asked, holding up the money, "do you think just the two is enough? Plus the change? I feel bad giving the rest away, since it's not my money. It really belongs to Mom."

"Yeah, *sure*," said Henry. "Just take *my* dollar and *Emma's* but keep your own money. *That* seems fair."

Despite Henry's grousing, they all agreed that two dollars should be plenty of sacrifice to gratify the spirits of the field, if there were such spirits. Last of all, Roy added the small white skull gently to the pile of money in the hole. It seemed right, since the mouse had likely been a field mouse. They all scrabbled the pile over with dirt.

When Henry's hand touched something hot and smooth, he jumped back. "Ow!" he yelped.

"What is it?" asked Emma.

Henry bent to pick up the hot something-or-other, then held it up so that they could all see. It was a large skeleton key the size of a teaspoon, so caked with dirt that none of them had noticed it lying camouflaged on the ground. Henry wiped it against his shirt, and as the dirt flaked off, everyone saw it was made of a bronzy kind of metal, with a rough surface and fancy scroll-work at the top.

"I guess it got hot in the sun and burned me," he said.

"Can I see it?" asked Roy.

"Sure," said Henry, handing it over. "But give it back. I want to keep it. It's mine."

Emma glanced at the key and then up at the wall. "Maybe it goes to the castle? It *looks* like a castle key."

Roy shook his head. "I don't think so. Whatever the wall used to be, even if it *was* a castle, it hasn't been in a long time. Any key to something so old would be long gone or buried deep underground by now." He handed the key back to Henry, who put it in his pocket.

"C'mon, guys," said Susan, bored with the key. "I'm thirsty. Let's think about heading back."

"But I want to finish the sacrifice," said Henry. He began to chant again and jump around.

"Fine." Susan relented. "But make it quick."

Henry jumped faster. He broke off a slender corn-stalk and waved it above his head, chanting even louder. Then he stopped for a second to ask, "Hey, who wants to say the great appreciation prayer while I do my native corn dance of thanks?"

"I will!" piped up Emma, who began to pray loudly and with great feeling.

"Dear Wall, we think you are a very nice wall and we would like you to be our wall from now on. We hope two dollars and some cents is enough because the rest really belongs to Mrs. Levy and it's all we have. Thank you very much and we'll come see you again soon and maybe we'll bring you another present someday. Something better than a dead mouse. Okay? The End. AMEN!" She shouted this last word at the top of her lungs, and when she was done, Emma brushed her hands together and blew a kiss toward the little mound.

It wasn't quite the ceremonial prayer Henry had envisioned, but everyone (trying not to laugh) said "Amen" too. When it was over, they walked around the wall together (even Susan, who had forgotten she was thirsty), taking note of their gigantic new possession. It did, for all the silliness of the ceremony, make it feel official; it felt more theirs now that they'd claimed it. Ritual has that effect.

And that was when Emma said, "Roy?"

And Roy answered, "Yeah?"

And Emma pulled him over by the hand and pointed. "I know you said it's not the right key to the castle, but doesn't it *look* like the castle wants a key?"

Roy leaned down, looked at where Emma was pointing, and admitted she was right. There, about three feet from the ground, on the shady side of the wall, was a very dingy keyhole set into a metal plate. The metal plate was exactly the same bronzy color as the key.

"Hey, Henry, bring that key back over here a minute," he called.

Henry stuck his head around the corner of the wall. "Why?" He joined them.

"Just because," said Roy, who stood up, took the key, and fitted it into the hole.

"What's happening?" Susan asked, walking over to hover over her brother's shoulder.

"Henry's key seems to fit this keyhole," said Roy, "which is weird. Don't you think?" He joggled the key.

Henry squatted by the metal plate. "I've never seen a key fit into a *wall* before. Usually there's a door or something. I mean, there's nothing for this to open, right?"

"Yeah, but it *does* fit," said Roy. "I even think it'll turn." He held his breath as he turned it.

They all listened to the heavy grinding sound and the rough click that it made. They all waited, but nothing more happened. There didn't appear to be anything to actually unlock.

Roy gave the key back to Henry.

"Fascinating." Susan yawned. "Anyway," she said, "I think that since we've claimed the wall and it's one-fourth mine, I'm going to use it for a rest." She walked a few yards over and plunked right down beside their bikes. She combed out her hair with her fingers, applied a coat of lip gloss, wiped a smear of dirt from her right knee, and then plucked a thick blade of grass, which she placed between her thumbs. When she blew on it, it produced a wonderful piercing sound. One by one, the others followed her lead, until they were all lined up between the metal plate and the bikes, whistling on blades of grass (except for Emma, who could only make a thpbtttttt sound when she blew).

"Dang," said Henry, looking up at the wall leaning over them. "It's not so bad once you're out of the sun, but now that I'm not so hot, I'm thirsty."

"Join the club," said Susan.

"Yeah," said Roy. "We should really have brought some water with us." Roy was usually prepared.

"Ooh," said Susan. "Water! I wish I had a big cold glass of water right now, with a lot of crushed ice and a lemon."

"Or better yet—some pop!" said Roy.

"Or a slushy?" said Emma. "A cherry-lime one."

"Or a root beer float!" said Henry.

Which caused everyone to make the same sound at once—the sound you make when someone else is enjoying something yummy and they don't offer to share.

"Mmm," said Susan wistfully. "A root beer float would be perfect. I *sooo* wish we were at Annabelle's Diner right now."

Then—in the space of a breath, a moment—they *were* at Annabelle's!

They were lined up in exactly the same formation, sitting in a row against a wall, only now the wall was made of slick, smooth tile instead of rough dark stone. Instead of the summer heat, they breathed in chilly air scented with frying hamburgers. Instead of the corn-fields, they looked up and saw a bustling room full of lunchtime diners and harried waitresses darting to and fro. Their bikes were there too, leaning against the wall beside them.

They all blinked. They all gasped. They all stared openmouthed at each other, but then a big voice boomed at them from above, from behind a cash register. "You kids know you can't bring them bikes in here. You better get 'em out fast. Before Annabelle sees ya. Now SCRAM!"

What else could they do? They scrammed! They hopped up and wheeled their bikes through the swinging doors that led to the street. They propped them up and sat down on a bench, stunned.

Finally Susan spoke. "What—just—happened?" she asked.

"No clue," said Henry.

Roy and Emma shrugged.

"Do you think anybody saw us?" asked Susan. "I mean, inside the diner. I mean, did they see us *appear?*"

"I don't *think* so," said Henry.

"It was loud and busy, and it's not the kind of place where people pay attention," explained Roy. "I guess."

At last Emma asked *the* question. "Was it . . . magic?"

Nobody answered her, so Emma tried again, a little louder. "I *said,* was it MAGIC?"

"It couldn't be, could it?!" said Susan. "Maybe it was an unexplained phenomenon, an optical illusion?" She spoke these words, but her face said something else. Her face, bright and flushed, said *Magic!*

"A what?" asked Emma.

Roy explained. "Susan means it's a kind of trick, Em. 'Illusion' is a word people use to explain things they can't figure out."

"But she doesn't mean it. Do you, Susan?" asked Henry.

"You really think this is magic, Roy?" asked Susan, turning to face him. "Actual magic?"

Roy pushed his bangs from his eyes and thought about this. "Like I said earlier, anything's possible. I don't know what we found, but I know we found something, and this feels like one time when thinking won't help. I have no idea what happened, but I'm not about to let this chance slip away. It wouldn't make any sense to waste it just because we don't *understand* it. Right?"

"Yeah!" said Henry excitedly. "Why not? What do we have to lose by trying?"

Emma bounced up and down on the bench beside him.

"Oh—my—gosh!" Susan was smiling broadly now, but then she bit her lip and added, "If any of you ever tell anyone else that I went along with this, that I *believed*—"

"What do you mean?" asked Emma. "What's wrong with *believing*?"

Henry had another thought. "Of *course* I won't tell anyone. Jeez! In fact, *nobody* can, or it'll be ruined. That's, like, the first rule of magic, isn't it? In all the books when you find a magic talisman, you don't tell *anyone.* Magic *has* to stay a secret." He was very serious about this.

Emma, who was just beginning to discover such wonderful books as *Magic by the Lake,* nodded solemnly.

"Now everyone swear," Henry said. "Swear that you won't tell a soul." Henry looked at each of them one by one. "Swear!"

Susan swore quickly, with a giggle.

Emma's eyes were gigantic as she repeated after Susan. Sacrifices and swearing all in one day!

Roy appeared cool and thoughtful. "I solemnly swear," he said, "though I reserve the right to revisit this issue at a later time, since we just don't know what'll happen. Okay?"

Henry gave a brief head shake that meant "Yes, okay, sure, whatever you say, Roy" and also "That won't happen, goofball" before he went on in a rush of excitement. "And I swear too. Okay! Now, do you realize what we have? We have a *wishing wall!*"